Run With the Hunted 3:
Standard Operating Procedure

Jennifer R. Donohue

This is a work of fiction. Names, characters, places, and incidents either are the product of the author's imagination or are used fictitiously. Any resemblance to actual persons, living or dead, events, or locales is entirely coincidental.

Run with the Hunted 3: Standard Operating Procedure © 2020 by Jennifer R. Donohue

Paperback ISBN: 9781945548130

Ebook ISBN: 9781945548123

For Jim

Chapter One

———

Right about when I find the right car, my robot dog's legs freeze up. Should've included it in the equipment breakdown last night; the desert grit out here doesn't agree with it at all, but I figured I had a little more time. The trip to Chiba is a long haul and a long wait once you're there. It's only the one guy who fixes 'em.

"Sorry bud," I say, and it blinks its luminous blue eyes at me and wags its tail.

The car's battery is dead, that's good. Means no security's gonna start blaring, painting a target in the local map. I can just break in old fashioned way, give it a jump with the handheld kit, and by then it'll figure that I'm supposed to be here and we can go on our way. When the cars still have power, Bits can cut the security and remote-start them for me, but that takes some of the fun out of it.

"Who are you talking to?" Bits says in my ear.

"The dog." Of course nobody's around; I'm just off a highway out of town, near one of those concrete block type of apartments that I'm not sure anybody's ever lived in.

It's not a super rare car I'm breaking into, a Jaguar but not limited run. People like buying the car of their dreams here, and then waking up and going home. I like taking the cars before the police impound them and selling them to somebody in the street racing circuit, after Bits hacks the keys and fixes up the registration records for us.

This one's in okay shape. Tires full, all dusty but the windows are closed. They're not always closed, sometimes you come out here and they've got a whole desert ecology on the inside. I slide the slimjim down in the driver's door, fish around, pop the lock. The keys're in the ignition, that means I won't have to hotwire first, fix later. I pull the hood release, tap the dog's head when I walk past it again. It does the quizzical hound head tilt that all the dogs we ran when I was a kid would do, if they were thinking about something. I guess the robot dog has more to think about than they did, and probably less. I'm not sure how good its sniffer is, for instance. I know what the specs say, just haven't seen it in action.

I check the fluids before I clip on the cables. Stuff's low but not awful; we got this one in the sweet spot. Not so tip-top that it's some kind of bait for a police sting, not so rock bottom that it wasn't worth it for me to walk out here. It starts like it has morning-after regrets, gravelly and hoarse, but it starts. I feel that. I unclip the equipment, put it and the dog in the passenger seat, walk around once to make sure all the lights light. I swap out license plates. "How we looking, Bitsy?"

"All clear," she says.

"All right then, see you in a little while." Seems like anytime I'm driving around here, there isn't much traffic, which doesn't make much sense. There are so many people here. I even sometimes just go a cafe or whatever by those tree island things they built, to watch the cars.

"Okay. Dinner's ready."

"Is it, now." She doesn't answer, probably got lost in the stars again or something. We kind of swap around with whose turn dinner is, every once in awhile go out with Bristol, who doesn't live here, but doesn't *not* live here. She skips around when she's inclined, which is a lot. It's a good leaping-off point for plenty of glamorous locales or whatever. I wasn't thinking about food but yeah, I could eat. I also want to get this car in the garage and Bits hooked up to its brain, and I want to get the robot dog broken down to see if it's grit, or something else.

I've probably only driven a Jag about five times, this trip included. It's a nice ride, a little too nice. Sometimes I do want to feel that connection to the road and not like I'm flyin' along on a cloud or something. Get too comfortable is when you make mistakes. I check my mirrors the way church people cross themselves. But nobody's following me, I don't see any cars more than once, I see a few cops but they're just doing normal cop things, no sweat. I pull into our garage next to the range rover, cut the engine, and get out to watch our street surveillance for a few minutes. That's normal; the way we work sometimes, paranoia's healthy. Still nothing, though, and I unpack the car before going upstairs.

Dinner tonight means that Bits ordered from a few delivery places; falafel and fast food and pastries apparently. The bags're all spread out on the counter, still closed, and she's sprawled on the couch, headset on. The TV is on too, tuned into some international news station, captions scrolling by in like five languages. There's a certain amount of background noise she likes running; hell, I do too, but I think we got different reasons for it. Mine's to do with coming from a big family, hers is to do with appreciating static like it's music.

"Hey the falafel place does cakes in jars so I got a bunch," she says, not moving.

"I'm gonna take the dog apart first, I'll eat later."

"Bristol's coming over later."

"Is that who the pastries're for?"

"Yeah, she's out to dinner right now."

"Perfect."

She sits up then, as I start down the hall, pushing her headset up. "What's wrong with the dog?"

"He stopped walking."

She makes a face. "Is it the sand, you think?"

"I'm hoping."

"Well, Chiba's always fun." Tech guts wonderland for her, she means. Some people travel places for street food, religious sites, art, Bits likes going places where she can rummage through bins of old tech and see what she can build. Sometimes it's like she's making stuff from the future that never happened, instead of the future we got. Less there to occupy me, though, especially with how jumpy Japan's gun laws are. Hong Kong, though, there's some good fun there. And who knows where Bristol would want to tra la la off to. Providing we go as a unit, of course. We all got our own tastes.

"We don't know yet that I need to go to Chiba."

"No." She shrugs, and I shrug, and I take the dog to my room. My workbench there is mostly for guns, but I've taken apart engine components there, and the robot dog. The garage is too small to really work in, it's a weird little building we're in that makes me think of row housing except it's freestanding. Like all those places back home that dried up and died out after the industry left, and they took down the houses one by one, sometimes built brick supports for the people who wouldn't vacate. It's hard, getting people to leave home, no matter how bad home seems to outsiders. Unless they're the type that never loved anything about home to begin with, like Bristol.

I stroke my hand over the dog's back, power him down. There's a little pattern puzzle to lift his backplate off and give you access to everything, so you don't do it accidentally. And yeah, there's some grit in there, but the problem looks to be the more fiddly bits of the drive train. It's more complicated than a drive train; all four legs move independently, in all the different dog gaits, but that's what it amounts to. I blow the grit out with some canned air, poke around to see if I can fix it anyway, and then figure I'll leave things in the hands of the professional robot dog fixing guy. There's too many circuit boards and chips and nice solder work in there, and even though I can mess around with basic ones thanks to Bits, these're above my paygrade.

Chiba it is, then. Maybe it's in the backyard of wherever Bristol wants to send us, because that's a lot of what we talk about when we get together, what we're gonna do next. I think we're all pretty set on funds, but they don't last forever, and it it ain't a great idea to get lazy and fall too far out of the game. I message the robot repair guy to get the ball rolling; no telling how long the wait'll be, any way you look at it. I leave the robot dog shut down. It won't know the difference, that way. Won't have to wonder why it can't walk.

I go hose off, since Bristol's like as not to comment on whether I stink, and by the time I'm done and dressed, I hear her high heels coming up the stairs. TV stays on though. She'd love to have device free dinners or whatever, but Bits likes having that little line of analog interference if somebody's driving past waving around listening devices. Can't say as I disagree.

Bristol's pink-cheeked like she went for the third drink instead of stopping at two, and bright eyed like she just won at her favorite game. She's got a bottle of wine with her, no surprise; she thinks none of the rest of us have any taste.

"What's the verdict?" Bits asks, like Bristol wasn't chattering about this or that, and Bristol pouts a little, picks up the remote to change the tv.

"Outside my expertise. I sent the guy a message."

"Whatever are you two going on about?" Bristol asks finally, channel now to her liking and rummaging for a corkscrew in the kitchenette drawers.

"The robot dog's busted."

"Oh darling, I'm sorry." She pauses, and I just grin at her, hard. She doesn't give a fuck about the robot dog. "Is tonight bad, shall I come back?"

"Nah, let's get things going."

"I *did* hope you would say that, and this little thing I've heard about might just help distract you from your dog worry."

I frown. "Like, 'cause we're getting to work or—"

"Because it has to do with *dogs*!" Bristol doesn't talk about animals much. Now that I think about it, I've never seen her interact with a single one, not even the robot dog. Not even somebody's way too expensive cat that lounges only on pillows and eats paté or whatever. I'm real sure she's never even ridden on a mechanical bull in a bar, and most of them don't even have heads. That kinda weirds me out actually; I've even seen Bits pet a dog at least once. Or look at a bird that flew by. Not Bristol.

"Dogs? Bristol, you don't *like* dogs. What're we gonna do that has to do with dogs?"

"I have never said that," she says primly, finally getting the cork out of the damn bottle and pouring one of those stemless unbreakable wine glasses half full. They're probably not actually unbreakable, but I haven't gotten bored enough to try it yet. Probably if you shoot one or run it over or whatever, it'll break. Video's probably online already, another missed chance. Shootin' stuff to see if it breaks. How it breaks? When it breaks. Everybody online copies everybody else anyway, I could find a niche. "And are you aware that there is a very exclusive, highly competitive market for some types of dog?"

"Breeds," Bits mutters, but not loud enough to interrupt.

"I may have been, yeah," I say. Not really, but it's not like I never been to an animal auction before.

"And do you know how much the most expensive dog has ever auctioned for?" We both just look at her. Bitsy's lookin' it up I'm sure, but there's no sense stealing Bristol's thunder at this stage of the game. "Five *million* dollars, just last year. Before that it was two million, around the turn of the century. They actually had quite the downturn after that for quite awhile, I'm not really sure what caused the resurgence. I'm sure it's a little like the stock market."

"Totally just like it," Bits says, somehow with a straight face.

"They what? Dogs? You're losin' me here, Bristles."

"Oh the breed of dog, I'm so sorry. The Tibetan Mastiff." She looks at us as though it's a big reveal, and Bits and I look at each other. Bristol sighs.

I give it a shot. "But so what's the deal? Like, if the Tibetan Mastiff market is so boom and bust, shouldn't we've bought low to sell high?"

"If we actually wanted much to do with those animals for any length of time," Bristol says and I just bray laughter. Like I said.

"But who would want that?" Bits asks, hiding a smile.

"Exactly! What I propose is much simpler."

"Y'know, Bristles, you always *think* that..." I say.

"One of my contacts in Tokyo can put me in touch with some-body who will pay three million dollars for a specific one of those dogs that is to go to auction next week. However, they can *only* pay three million dollars, so they want to hire some-body to just...scoop the dog up for them."

"Scoop up the—now I'm no dog expert, but most of the time, a dog's got mastiff in the name it's a pretty big dog."

Bristol waves her non-wine holding hand. "It's a *puppy* how big could it be? And we know how easy it is to get into places and walk away with all manner of things. This would probably be the easiest three million dollars we ever make."

"I dunno, the Paris job was pretty easy." Plus the appeal of bein' able to say the Paris job.

Bristol rolls her eyes. "And significantly less than three million dollars."

"In today's exchange," Bits points out.

"Yeah we're not exactly strapped for cash," I say. "Not enough to do something you hate."

"I wouldn't ask us to do something I *hate*." Bristol's starting to get pouty. "I'm not a monster, I don't hate *puppies*."

"You probably haven't spent much time with puppies, they're the monsters." I laugh and she sighs gustily. "Okay, okay, fine tell us more. Where's the dog now? Where's the auction gonna be?"

"The auction will be in Macau, I don't know where the dog is right this second."

"Macau? You sure you don't wanna just do a little casino job instead of this dognapping thing? That's what all those movies you like are, right? Casino jobs?" They're fun movies, anyway. Too big a team though.

"We don't have enough people for a casino job," she says, sipping her wine. "No I think this will be good, a little diversion from your gearhead games, and then we can come back here, I think, or do whatever."

Come back here meaning the location isn't burned yet, yeah. But... "Bristol, is somethin' going on that makes you want to blow town for a little while?"

"I don't know what would make you ask that." She looks at me with big innocent eyes. "I've heard of a job I think will suit us, in a location that's favorable. Macau is rather near where you take the robot dog for repair, isn't it?" I shake my head. It's closer than here but it ain't exactly next door. Bristol sighs. "Fine, but you would have been leaving town yourself in a few days anyway, wouldn't you?"

"You got me there." She isn't lying but she isn't telling the truth. But, good enough for now. "Bits, what do you think?"

"It sounds easy which means something terrible will happen," she says cheerfully. "Let's do it."

Chapter Two

The thing about flying is you have to do it without a weapon, and I hate traveling without a weapon. I do always know how to find one once I'm where I'm going, and I think about this every time too. I learned in school a million years ago, or maybe Bits saw it on the internet and showed me, that squirrels don't exactly remember where they've hidden stuff. Squirrels just know the types of places where stuff is likely to be hidden. And that's how it is for me; it isn't that I got guns hidden globally, I just figure out where guns are likely to be hidden. And I return the favor, hide new stuff when I'm flush, say thanks to whoever when I'm in need. Let the circle be unbroken, by and by lord, by and by. And especially lately, I been flush a lot, so I restock those places. It's like little free libraries.

Plus, nowadays, you go to the right places, you can get enough parts 3D printed that're innocuous enough by themselves but put 'em together and you got a handgun that walks right through security scans. Not great when just anybody can do it, there's a lotta folks out there just want to hurt people for the sake of it, and there's no way to trust that equipment the way you can with actual brands. Real brands, you know if something's a piece of shit that's gonna melt by your seventy fifth round, or that you can leave in a puddle for six months, slap a mag in it, and fire it without even shaking out the barrel. I guess I'm glad I can reach for the tech when I need it. If I was a computer nut like Bits, I'd probably set myself up with a bun-

13

cha the printers, do a bespoke gun boutique, but I don't got the patience with the electronics or the eye for design. I can fix motors and maintain my equipment, and that's all I need. The robot dog would say otherwise, I guess, but I *didn't* get the talking version for a reason.

My Japanese ain't great but most people at the airport speak English. Hell, it seems like most non Americans speak more than one language, English included. My school was barely a school anymore by the time I got there, it's not like we had language classes, and it's not something I pick up easy the way Bits and Bristol do. I try, though, and I smile big, and even out in the street, seems like most people like trying to help the big dumb American who isn't an asshole. Especially if they recognize the carrying case for the robot dog. People get real sympathetic then, which is kinda weird, since I know there's only so many people had access to this model, but when you're a legend, you're a legend, and the guy in Chiba is a legend.

It's pretty much impossible for him to be the same guy in Chiba that's been there since the early oughts when the first kind of these robot dogs were breaking down and there was only one guy left, and that occupies my thoughts a lot. Did the shop get passed to him, like when a venerable sushi chef passes the restaurant down to his son that he's trained his whole life, once he's absofuckinglutely certain that he can do the job right, knows every aspect of the craftsmanship? (I watched a documentary okay) I guess maybe. Not like I know enough Japanese to ask, and besides, seems like it'd be rude. It's none of my beeswax. I give him money, he fixes my dog, and that's all we need to be to each other.

Anyway, plane food's garbage and that's me saying that, so it's gotta be real bad. It'll be an easy thing to stop for street food once I drop the dog off. Chiba's got a famous monorail, and even though it's a ride, that's what I take from the airport just for the sake of it. I don't like taking the trains stateside, not the hyperloop either. Other places, it's one hundred percent the way to go. In America, I just always want the great American road trip, I guess. Like sure, as a nation, we were historically *really* into trains, but then the car happened and then the highways happened and freedom is the open road, blah blah blah. The open road ain't so great if you've got a flat tire or drones after you, but it's the risk I take over and over again. Beats old fashioned action star running on the top of the train bullshit. Which isn't to say I wouldn't if I had to. Maybe I'd want the equipment for it, though. Like magnet boots. Are the tops of trains magnetic? Guess you wouldn't wanna risk that on a maglev train though.

At some point, probably in the 'oh god we're really fucking the climate here and we're actually going to do something about it' frenzy, a lot of cities, worldwide, went back to what they once were, trollies and trams and people on foot. Definitely after the pandemic. But no cars means the roads can be narrower, means there's a lot more little businesses, and a lot more people in the streets, which I think are made of that kinetic rubber stuff that gathers power and transfers it to the street lights, the air conditioners, the surveillance.

It's cold enough that it's fine for me to wear a hood up, and at this point all of my hooded things have the flashy material in the fabric, to fuck with the cameras. I think all of Bits's clothes in general have that. And Bristol loves those 1900s starlet going for a ride in a convertible roadster scarves. Plus I feel like she was chattering about her foundation or some shit having stuff in it that was transparent to the naked eye and didn't affect her look, but fucked with being photographed. She does love being photographed; she does not like bein' in custody. None of us do, but she's the one with the most recent taste of that. She went on to Macau first though, to get a sweet suite with a view that she prefers or something. Maybe get in some spa time.

We all traveled separate. I'm a little surprised, not-surprised, that Bits didn't come with me, actually, but I figure she just wants to worm her way into all the security soon as possible. Anyway, international like this, it's better to arrive separate, but stay in touch. If she wants, she can probably be in any of these cameras to see what I'm up to. Or hack the little toy drones that this street vendor guy has, to have a look around. It's weird, after this time, to just be walking around without somebody here watching my back. I'd probably never *say* that to Bits and definitely not to Bristol, that I like having them back me up. We work together well, each doing our part. We don't need to say it. We just keep on doing it.

My connecting flight to Macau is in four hours, so I don't have a whole lot of turnaround time. Don't need to find a walka-round weapon while I'm here, I'm just like any civilian who wants their goddamn robot dog to just work the way that it's supposed to. I get to the shop and it's the same as it's been my other two trips. How many Americans make the trip, I wonder? Still. It's not like I'm Bits and just want to be as invisible and unmemorable as possible, I don't care about that, but it's a thought that I put on the shelf in my mind, that if any of the pissed-off government agents looking for any of us happened to come here, I could be identified, and that'd be another pin on their map.

Because I messaged ahead, they have the work order all filled out for me, even have some diagnostic guesses in English, and I'm able to tell them which ones I already tried. The young man who goes over it with me blinks a lot behind his glasses, and seems very thoughtful. I'm not the kind of person you want to have a misunderstanding with, even though I'm definitely on my best behavior here. Real polite, please and thank you, though there's no reason not to have manners in stores and things. Service staff, they don't deserve whatever bullshit's happening in your life.

//How'd it go?// Bits messages me when I'm back on the street.

//Fine as can be expected// I say. //It'll be ready by the time I'm back.//

//Is this...does this seem weird?//

//Bristol's job? Sure does, but you were all for it.//

//I was worried you were getting bored.//

//Oh you'd know if I was getting bored.// I grin, and somebody on the sidewalk moves out of my way a little more vigorously than they needed to. Whoops.

//No I mean, I noticed you were getting bored and I was worried about it.//

//You didn't say anything!//

//It's hard to say some things,// she says, and fair enough.

//We'll talk about it at the hotel.// I think about it. //We'll have what, a day or two, between us and the auction? Plenty of time to figure logistics and get more out of Bristol. Maybe this dog has a diamond collar or something, and that's what she really wants.//

//You'd think she'd have had enough of diamonds.//

//Bristol? Enough of diamonds?// I laugh, and some people turn their heads and look at me. Too loud again.

//Well remember, she won't wear them until she's *old*, which sounds like she stole it from a movie.//

//She did steal it from a movie, we watched it, remember? And she thinks 'old' is forty.// I go to one of the ramen vending machines instead of a stand; nothing's wrong, that I can tell, but I just have a feeling that I shouldn't spend any more time than I need to, not now that I've been getting people's attention. No telling who you might run into. Maybe a friend, maybe not a friend. Or maybe not a friend anymore. I burn as few bridges as possible, a lot fucking fewer than Bristol, who I think maybe set her whole old life on fire before she walked away without turning back like some kinda action hero. But it's been a couple. Plus you never know when the government'll change its mind about not needin' you anymore and just whistle Lassie

Come-Home and because of whatever they programmed you and injected you and implanted you with, you just gotta do it. As far as I know, I'm all good and deprogrammed, especially after that last roadtrip stateside, but that's kinda the whole point. You don't actually know.

That tension goes away once I'm back on the train to the monorail so. There's something to be said for following your instincts. Or I just imagined the whole thing, and it'll never matter.

Chapter Three

===

I'm one hundred percent certain that literally anyplace else in Macau is cheaper than the Venetian. It's damned impressive, I'll give 'em that. A Michelin starred restaurant, of course, Bristol loves that shit. Chock full of suites, that's good, the more breathing room we can give each other when we're on a job, the better. They've also got a big goddamn shopping mall with a McDonald's and a Uniqlo and a hundred other things and I'll bet that just sticks in her craw to see. They're really committed to the whole aesthetic, though, It occurs to me that maybe Bristol picked this place because she thinks Bits'll like it. Like, there's a place with an Eiffel Tower right down the street, she could've picked that and didn't. One of these days I'll have to ask her how many Eiffel Tower proposals she's gotten.

I take the elevator up to the top floor, because I guess she couldn't resist the notion of going all the way to the top. The hotel is real quiet, not like every cheap joint I've picked. Must mean that the walls are thick enough to actually have real art hung on them, or real copies of real art, maybe even with wood frames instead of wood-look recycled plastic, and the carpet is plush enough that even when I try to stomp like a fairytale giant, my footsteps are swallowed up. If there's people sittin' and looking at the security cameras, they're probably laughing. Or Bits is already in the machine, and they're just looking at a loop of the last time the hallway was empty on repeat, with the time-stamp advancing the way anybody would expect it to. She always erases our footsteps behind us, like when horses are dragging branches in an old cowboy movie.

I get to our door and don't even have to wave my key at it, it's unlocked, and I push it open to a room nicer than I've ever owned, with a view across the city to the harbor. I wonder if all those windows open, and honestly pray that it never matters; this is pretty far up, and there ain't a lot that I'm afraid of, but it doesn't mean I wanna free climb down the side of this bitch either.

Bristol is pacing back and forth on the phone with somebody, speaking French and making faces so that her tone of voice comes out right. Like, everybody knows that when you smile on the phone, people hear the smile in your voice or whatever, but she takes it to a whole 'nother level. Bits is swallowed up on one of the couches, cushions galore, and the window-sized TV is tuned to the weather channel but has a feed of local news layered over the bottom corner. TV's've been doing that about forever now but you hardly ever see anybody use the in-picture thing. I drop my bag from a little higher up than I need to and Bristol turns and raises her eyebrows at me. I grin and wave, and she rolls her eyes and vanishes into one of the rooms, the door closing, whisper-quiet. This whole quiet hotel thing is gonna get to me real quick.

"How was your flight?" Bits asks.

"It was great, I got bumped to first class after Chiba, so they gave me drinks in a glass like a real grownup. Lemon scented hot towels. Dessert." I flop on the couch next to her, put my boots up on the coffee table. I probably should've grabbed something outta the minifridge first. Or no, those things cost a bajillion dollars. But I didn't notice any vending machines either. There's a point at which hotels class themselves outta having a vending machine on any of the floors and I just think that's really sad. Probably no ice machines either, they're all in the rooms. Places really lose character when they take out those little common area touches, capsule everything off. "We got a timeline yet?"

"Yes and no? The auction's just a few blocks away, and the objects being auctioned, which are not all ridiculously expensive dogs, have been arriving for a week or more. Bristol's trying to figure out if our target is here yet." She glances at me, smiling a little.

"Well is it?"

"Yeah."

I laugh. "Well did you tell her?"

"You know she doesn't like being interrupted on the phone." She laughs too. Of course Bits would have the intel; once she had access to the auction catalog, I'm sure she was tracing the dog's owner, the dog's handler, the dog's seller, the flight manifests, so many numbers that it just makes my brain swim but she's really in her element.

"I think we're all a little bit jumpy about that. How many times have good things happened when Bristol was on the phone?"

"I'm sure plenty, but the bad ones stick out."

"Ain't that the truth." I get up and look out a window; 38 floors. I wonder if hotels still have that superstition about having or not having a thirteenth floor; I didn't notice it when I was in the elevator and it would be too weird for me to go back out and check. Maybe that's a Western thing anyway, different cultures have different lucky and unlucky numbers. Different lucky and unlucky colors. And animals.

"Dolly, hello! And here we gather!" I wonder sometimes what Bristol's original accent was, because the way she talks now isn't how anybody talks. Not outside of old movies, like that one I found and then made Bits watch with me because the main character was just one hundred percent Bristol, she had to've seen the movie and done it on purpose, there's no other explanation. But that's part of the point. We don't ask each other for explanations like that. We're the people we are, not the people we came from. Just some of us changed a little more than others, I think. I don't think I changed much at all.

"We sure do! And we're starving, actually. Were you getting us room service?"

"You're always starving." She comes and perches on the edge of one of the overstuffed chairs, and I lean way over and pull a bottle of water from the minifridge just to watch her flinch a little. She's real good at hiding it. But also I'm sure there's only so much real money we're paying for this place anyway. And there's only so real money seems, after awhile.

"Fair enough. What's our plan?"

"Well, I have secured my place at the auction," she says.

"Oh your paddle number?"

Bits snickers and Bristol stares at me. "My what?"

"Don't you get a little fan or paddle or something that you wave when you bid? That'll have a number on it."

"I don't...think they call it that, no."

"So you don't have one."

"Nobody said anything about *paddles*, no." She's fun to rile up, but I gotta be careful not to take it too far.

"Okay okay so you're going into the auction through the front door. Then what, you're just gonna pretend to have the cash or whatever to outbid everybody for the dog?" It's possible that she just actually has enough money saved to outright buy the dog, but if that was the case, then we wouldn't be here and laying out a plan to steal the dog and collect a smaller paycheck than its pricetag.

"Yes, and then once I have access to that back auction area, where the goods are kept, I can let you two in and we can make off with the animal."

Carefully, Bits says "Don't you think that's making things a little more complicated than they need to be?"

"Well we need to make sure it's the right dog, don't we?"

"They probably number 'em or something." I open the fridge again and look at what's in there. Lots of little snacky things, absolutely none of it prefab like an American hotel that would have like, Snickers bars and stuff. White Claws. "Collars? Tags? Chips?"

Bristol waves her hand. "Regardless, yes, that's the plan. We'll have to rent a car of course, and be careful of the interior color, to mitigate the dog hair."

"And then we're taking the dog right to your buyer?"

"Well of course, it isn't as though we have anywhere to *keep* it. And I don't know the first thing about keeping a dog."

"So just a grab and go, that's not so bad," I say. Other than Bristol's insistence on being right there with her face in the action. I'm going to have to take a little walk and get some equipment. Bits and I share a glance, and I think she has more ideas than just about the color of the upholstery. Which, good, 'cause so do I.

Chapter Four

"She just always has to be *seen*," Bits says later, when Bristol is out auction shoes-and-dress shopping and we're eating fast food that we snuck off to get.

"It did work for the diamonds thing."

"Yeah, it's worked for things. But we *really* don't always need to be so high profile. We don't always need to have any kind of discernible profile. We could try that."

"Just in and out the back door with the dog after hours? Before or after the auction?" I guess I don't really have what people call a palate, but damn if fresh hot french fries aren't one of the best things in the world.

She shrugs. "Before for a lot of reasons, but also if Bristol's sudden appearance alerts INTERPOL or whatever, we can already be packed and leaving."

"Makes sense. Really, I just always assume Bristol's sudden appearance is gonna cause a problem, whether people know her or not."

Bits laughs. "I think she thinks that about you."

"Prob'ly." I laugh too, eat some more fries. "We gotta be prepared for her to be dramatic about this, like it's the ultimate betrayal."

"I think that's a risk I'm willing to take," Bits says thoughtfully. Bristol dramatics are just part of the package; there's no harm in it. Hell, she's as solid as any one of us, getting arrested on purpose and giving me time to go plug Bitsy into her rig in the hopes that her brain would stop coming outta her ears. And so I could get a new arm slapped on. Only some of that is exaggerated. Goddamn that was scary. Like. Top five. Just that whole bucket of snakes. I been shot, stabbed, lightly singed, shocked, partly drowned...but that's my first actual loss of limb. The skin's real skin at least, they tank grew that and grafted it on, so I don't have to worry about dust getting in or whatever.

And maybe it's better that I can't access my arm's biomechanical innards just to tinker around a little. Tempting though it is, even I know it's not really the best idea. I can't even fix my own robot dog. Tempting. Though actually the idea of opening a little door or whatever in my wrist or forearm so that I can get to fuses and stuff kinda freaks me out. There aren't fuses. It actually runs though my own generated bioelectricity or whatever. There's a manual that I've kinda skimmed. I know some people kinda hack them anyway, somehow, override the controls so they can get more strength out of them, or speed. It's tempting. Not the kind of decision you want to make in the middle of crisis, or the kind of thing you can just flip a switch on and get results. I don't think. Where is that manual? Maybe I should get a spare to tinker with first, get comfortable with it, then get a door put in.

"Okay. So we get the layout of the place, we figure where the cameras are. We pull the vehicle around, get inside between security sweeps, get the dog, get out, get back here. Much simpler. Much less risk. Plus, I still got that camouflage we pulled off that fed or whatever. When we recovered Bristol." She hesitates just a sec, then nods.

"Oh good. And I've got the layout of the place." She swipes the file over to me. "And I've got the auction catalog, but Bristol still has to tell us which dog's the right one."

"There's more than one dog at the auction? I assumed it was mostly gonna be art and shit."

"It is, but there's three dogs."

"You said the dog was here though?"

Bits blinks. "Yeah. All three dogs are here."

I take a sec to look at the pictures of the dogs. They might be puppies but they're the partly grown style of puppy, not the tumbly ball of fluff style of puppy. "So, what do you figure the point of stealing one of these guys is? Can't breed it legally, like registered, if you don't got the papers right?"

"Maybe breeding isn't the point." Bits looks off into the middle distance for awhile, probably reading something in AR. I always assume she's got at least three screens going at any given moment. Maybe one of those set it and forget it kinda games. Maybe she's keeping track of bitcoin mining, though I dunno where she'd have the rig for that set up. It wasn't at her place in Mexico. I think she sold that anyway. But I'm just making stuff up in my head to pass the time. "Anyway, if she doesn't tell us, I can just hack her email or whatever to see."

I frown. "I don't wanna start doing shit like that to each other. We'll just ask her. Show dogs always have weird names, don't they? She'll wanna giggle over that."

"Yeah maybe. You're probably right." Bits looks at me again. "Sorry. It just seems so simple sometimes. Like, a lot simpler."

"No harm, no foul." I clear the garbage, stuff it into the too-small garbage can, like the hotel people expect the rich folks using the suite to not generate very much garbage at all. You'd think they'd know better, dealin' with rich folks literally all the time. Rich folks throw everything away, and this is just paper stuff and there still isn't enough room. Makes me wonder how often room service comes up, actually. "Hey we should hang a thinger on the door. Do not disturb, no room service, whatever."

"You're right."

"And anyway, I'll bet the room is no pets." I keep a straight face until Bits kind of tilts her head quizzically and then I start snickering. We're both laughing when the door chimes softly and Bristol comes in with an armful of shopping bags.

"I'm sorry to have missed the joke, darlings."

"Aw, it's not a big deal," I say. "Was this just an excuse for a shopping trip?"

"Everything's an excuse for a shopping trip," Bits says, and Bristol pouts.

"I'd prefer if you two didn't gang up on me."

"Sorry Bristles," I say in an approximation of sincerity. She inhales, nostrils quivering visibly, and then smiles. Practiced, serene.

"Thank you, Dolly."

"Show us what you got?" I ask, not 'cause I really care much but because it'll perk her up and make her chatter about all kinds of things, guaranteed. And she does, and me and Bits pay part attention to that and I pay part attention to looking at the stuff Bits forwards me, a rental car company first and then intel on Tibetan mastiffs. Male or female, depending on how close to full sized, we're lookin' at something like seventy five to a hundred and fifty pounds, which is like a person but not unmanageable. I've wrangled more weight than that, especially since the body mods I got courtesy of Uncle Sam before the program ended and we all scattered. Even before my fuckin' arm got blown to pieces and I got a new one, just like the original only better.

"What do you think?" Bristol asks finally. She doesn't really care what either of us thinks, but it's just in her programming.

"I like the shoes with the red," I say. The shoes have red soles, like she walked through paint, or a whole lotta blood. Maybe there's some symbolism there; we only know so much of each other's stories, by design. "And that blue dress."

"Thank you," she says, smiling. "I've wanted a pair of shoes like that for a long time, actually."

"Why'd you wait? Not like you didn't have the money." That's like me craving a particular gun and not getting it. Not that I worry overmuch about brands, just functions.

She smiles a little, shrugs. She has her answer rehearsed and it's real funny to realize and watch that in action. "I suppose not, but it just didn't feel right before now."

"So happy to be able to share this joyous occasion with you," I drawl on purpose and if we were little kids she'd stick her tongue out at me.

"You could use a new pair of shoes, you know," she says huffily, packing her things away again.

"Yeah but I just got these ones nice and broken in," I say, looking down at my scuffed boots, raveling lace-ends, and Bits laughs. "Anyway, wouldn't want to steal any of your thunder, Bristles." She looks at me and I grin wickedly, waiting for her rebuttal. She fights with herself about it, visibly, and then takes her shopping bags to her room.

"Careful, she'll come up with a plan where we all need to dress nice," Bits says.

"She can come up with whatever plans she wants, doesn't mean we're doing 'em," I say. Bits makes worried "she'll hear you" eyebrows at me but honestly, we had a great plan for the diamonds that she reworked for the hell of it, and claimed that it was in the interests of making things quieter and safer. That's all me and Bitsy are doing, trying to keep things quieter and safer.

Chapter Five

———

Bits and Bristol're asleep when I go for my supply run. Well. Calm late night stroll. Seems like a lotta places, the only people out are taxis and rideshares and people stumbling home from bars or whatever. Taking a bus, which I also do. Here, though, there's a twenty four hour life, especially with the casino. They do some kind of road race here coupla times a year, and it's amazing they make it as glitzy as they do. Macau and Monaco, but here I think they have a motorcycle one and now a bullshit hovervehicle one but that stuff's still mostly prototype and not really in general circulation, in a way different from just not having enough money keeps stuff out of people's hands. They really hover, they're not like those self balancing skateboard things from the early aughts.

Nobody seems to pay much attention to me as I walk, and I don't get that feeling I had back in Chiba. I still gotta mention that to Bits, but I'm sure she's already doing whatever internet magic it is that she does to see who's where and who's talking to who and about what. It's always reasonable to assume we're on somebody's docket, at this point.

There's a lot more drones here than in other places, not just traffic cameras, but their patterns're predictable and recognizable, if they're just on auto. I don't see any that aren't. I can hear parties going on, some engines revving. Active race or not, some people like to speed run city streets at night. Can't say I've never done it, and it can be a way to make some fast cash.

I make my likely stops, collect a few things that fit in pockets or hidden holsters, nothing traceable that I can tell but I'll have Bits check that too. Ammunition, and a good workhorse hand-gun, a 1911 style that's god knows how old but taken care of so well that I almost don't take it. This is, or was, somebody's baby, a natural extension of their arm. But I need it, so I do take it, and hopefully I can leave it back where I found it after this. Hopefully it doesn't have to find its way to the end of my arm through any of this. A pair of tasers that looks like they've been fooled with to give off a bigger zap. We've already all got our riot gear, at least we don't need to worry about getting that together again from scratch. What variation Bristol wears of it is another story, but she's a grownup, there's only so much I can do about that. Riot gear sure didn't keep me from losing an arm.

As I circle back to the hotel again, I stop at a 7-Eleven for some junky heat lamp food that I can eat in peace, without Bristol's complete and utter disdain. 7-Elevens are an interesting place, same brand in Macau as in New Jersey as in Tokyo as in Paris, they're good at keeping things familiar, but there's only so familiar they can stay past a certain point. Okay maybe there isn't a 7-Eleven in Paris but I've made my point. And I love it, really I do. There's a Japanese restaurant across the street with a sushi bar and everything, but by the time the other two're eating breakfast, Bristol would turn her nose up at overnight sushi. Bits wouldn't mind, but Bits likes 7-Eleven just fine too, and I grab her some snack food bags with labels in varying languages. Cricket chips and seaweed snacks and something with cheese, I think.

The clerk is playing a game in AR, I know the signs after all this time with Bits, and besides, they've got the glasses for it. They ring me up without looking at me much, which is probably also just a self defense mechanism of working at a place like this overnight. The clerks at off-highway places back home had that same look, always. Maybe clerks at places like that in general. Lord knows they're thankless, low-paying jobs. But a job's a job, sometimes. You can't always do what me and Bits and Bristol do. Maybe they get health insurance. Most countries got laws about that kinda thing nowadays. Huh. Wonder if I have health insurance. Probably my replacement arm's better than health insurance would've gotten me anyway. Or I got it sooner, anyway; VA takes forever.

I grab the bus back over the bridge, take in the sights. Mainland China is right there, and there's a twisty-looking skyscraper that has a light show on the outside of it. The colors and patterns change something like ten times, and I wonder what that looks like from the inside. Probably like nothing, it's probably just color-changey on the outside, not like living inside an aquarium. I'm the only one who gets off when the bus stops, and I take an indirect walk back to the Venetian, eyeing the other casinos and idly thinking about what a real casino job would be like.

The cage is always in the middle of the floor, that's not gonna work when things're open unless you're a comic book villain. The vaults, those movies covered vault stuff. I'm not super in-

terested in vault stuff. We could hijack an armored car, that'd
be workable. That's happened, in the real world, and people've
gotten away with it. It's happened in the movies and gone hor-
ribly wrong, of course. Wouldn't be an interesting story if stuff
didn't go wrong. Anyway, money's *heavy*, and I'm sorry to say
there's only so much of it we could physically handle quickly.
Bristol might be stronger'n she looks, I dunno, but Bits definitely isn't.

Also, one of the other hotels in town has a ferris wheel on the
roof and I'm kinda mad at Bristol for robbing us of that oppor-
tunity. Maybe she's ferris wheel averse. Maybe she got engaged
to her one true love on top of a ferris wheel and then tragedy
struck, and that's why she's so familiar-but-distant with people
now. Probably not. My brothers used to try and scare me and
my sisters when we were little, shaking the cars on the ferris
wheel when we were at the top, except I didn't scare. My sisters,
though, they'd shriek and beg the boys to stop, and we'd all be
laughing and the operator down the bottom would yell at us to
stop. After awhile there weren't many fairs that came through
with rides, but we went to every damn one. Every, *every* fair,
even if there weren't rides and funnel cake and rigged games,
just barns of animals to look at that the 4H-ers threw their
whole damn lives into, coming to school ragged on every edge
during lambing season, after mucking stalls, after...doing whatever it is you do to care for pigs. The ones raising chickens and
things were pretty okay.

We never did livestock. You can't really count bees as livestock,
I don't think. But we had bees and were shadetree mechanics
for about forever, did some scavenging all over and machined

parts besides. We being my family. We check in every once in awhile, those of us who're left. We're doing okay. Nobody's been home in a long time. I thought about swingin' by when we were doing the decommissioned sites thing but then that went so far sideways we didn't know up from down. We being me and Bits and Bristol.

All's quiet in the hotel lobby when I walk back in. I forgot a reusable bag, normally I'll have at least one rolled up in a pocket but not while I'm flying I guess, so I had to buy one from 7-Eleven and just flaunt my shame to everybody. Everybody who cared, anyway; the lobby was empty of people to turn their noses up at me. The night shift dude wasn't even there, but he was when I left, and I had a paranoid moment that something was very wrong but then I heard a door close, and another one, and he appeared from some behind-the-desk door to find me standing there in his nice lobby in my combat boots, holding my 7-Eleven bag, and we had a long moment of looking at each other before I grinned at him and said "Have a good night" and he nodded and said "You too."

I guess it's not paranoia if you've got people after you on the regular. Still though. I take the stairs, not the elevator, all the way up. I stop and stretch at the landings, do pushups at a couple of them, run up some of the flights. Nothing says we're gonna be cooped up for awhile, but I get the feeling we're gonna be cooped up for awhile, and that's no good.

I forgot to check for the goddamn thirteenth floor again.

There's no sign anybody's done anything in the suite while I've been gone, and I maybe expected Bits to circulate a little bit because god knows what her internal clock's doing, but I hang the 'Do Not Disturb' on the door before I set the bolt and then jam a doorstop underneath. Then I hit the hay.

Chapter Six

===

We're getting about to auction day and Bits and I know the layout of the auction place, we know the pattern of the security patrols, we know how many people are there on the late shift, but we still don't know which goddamn dog it is. In the catalog, two are male, and one is female, and from their pictures I'm not sure I'd even say they're the same type of dogs, but dogs're hardly my specialty. And even if they were, it wouldn't be Tibetan Mastiffs, it'd be like. Catahoulas or Red-bone hounds.

"We could just ask her," I say.

"I could just break into her phone," Bits says. It's on the counter of the suite's kitchenette, an unprecedented abandonment, while Bristol's at one of the spas. I think that's where she is, anyway.

"Don't break into her phone, we already talked about this. We gotta trust each other at least a little, right."

She sighs. "We gotta trust each other a lot."

"We'll figure it out. Put a dog show on TV or something for when she comes back."

"What will *that* do?"

"I dunno, make her talk about it? She's the manipulator, not me."

"We're all manipulators," Bits grumbles.

"Then what's the problem?" I laugh. I've got my new and/or temporary handgun taken apart at the coffee table and all laid out on a nice cloth. It's pristine, it's like a me of the past or a possible me of the future left it there, it's just a pleasure to work with. I'm not gonna start thinking about time travel bullshit, though, it's hard enough wrapping my head around some of the knots that Bits ties her brain into when she's super deep into the computer side of thing. "Oh hey did you look at the zappers?"

"Yeah they look fine," she said. "Turned up, like you thought. Really clever how they did it, actually, you wouldn't think you'd be able to get more juice out of one of those. Like they'd have all you could have." She pauses and I almost ask if it's the settings and I wait. "Of course, as it turns out, there are settings that limit it. That's how they keep the production costs down, there's really only one device, but the stronger one is for professionals, and they gate the voltage for civilians."

"Kinda like how on some semi-autos, all you need's a paperclip and some know-how to make 'em rock and roll."

"...yeah. Like that."

Clearly, we got our own niche interests. "Anyways, when she comes back we should just—"

The door chimes and Bristol comes in, checks her phone, and in about thirty seconds she's talking on it in French. Bits watches her flounce back and forth, I put the gun back together. I'm not the type who names my guns, but I wonder if its old owner did that. Am I using somebody's Matilda? I don't know what people name their guns. Somebody's Bruce? Hell I never even named the robot dog. There was a name sharpied on the white plastic when I got it, but I cleaned that off of there. Didn't seem necessary. Names are a funny thing anyway, though. None of us go by our real names, right? Birth names? Whatever you might call 'em.

"Problem?" I ask when Brisol sets her phone down and sighs.

"Our buyer is *exceedingly* nervous, or his intermediary is, and requires much reassurance. I did soothe his nerves, I think, and everything is still set. I just cannot conceive of why people cannot maintain a professional demeanor."

"Wonder what made him nervous," I say. "Something seem wrong with the dog?"

"No, that I've heard, she's just fine," Bristol says distractedly, looking in the mini fridge. "Oh I'm just going to be wicked and have one of these awful little wine coolers."

"You devil you." I holster the gun, tilt my head at Bitsy. She nods just slightly; she caught that. "Why deny yourself, anyway?"

"It isn't special if you make it into a habit." She comes and arranges herself on one of the wingback chairs. "What have you two been up to?"

"Weapons checks," I say.

"Maps and security," Bits says.

Bristol nods and sips the wine cooler and I get up and get a beer and then say "Bristles, should we have any dog stuff on hand? At least a leash right?"

She thinks about it a moment. "Well, I would think they'd have a leash and other...equipment right there. The handlers have been caring for it, after all. And we'll be going from the auction to the intermediary, so we don't really need anything at all, I don't think."

"Roger that." Bits looks and me, and I shrug. Probably, yeah, there's leashes or whatever there, but I'm also at least gonna put some hot dogs in my pocket. I'm pretty sure dogs don't like just going with strangers. I could be wrong, this could be a baby show dog who's used to being handed off to whoever. Maybe somewhere in the middle. "So we're golden, then, we just wait."

"We just wait," Bristol agrees.

"You, uh, you wanna talk about why you wanted to leave Dubai?" I ask. Bristol kind of waves her free hand dismissively.

"My skin was getting so *dry*, I'm constantly amazed at how adaptable you all always are. And I'd heard about the spas here being a world class experience but for less than you might pay in Europe." I'd say she was blowing smoke but she seems serious. Really, if Bristol's talking she's lying in some way or another, even though we got a rule about that, so there *might* be something bothering her other than dry skin, but dry skin's on the list too.

"Is that where you've been all day, the spa?"

"Are you going to get one of those fish pedicures?" Bits asks with what seems like genuine interest.

Bristol visibly shudders. "I am not."

"Fish pedicure?"

"Yeah, I guess instead of them using the foot grater thing on you, you stick your feet in a pond and fish eat the dead skin. Or maybe they use the grater to loosen the skin first, I don't really know." Bits looks at Bristol for help, and Bristol just raises her eyebrows and takes another sip of her wine cooler. "Anyway. It's expensive and kind of specialty."

"Oh it sounds special all right," I laugh.

"Dolly, you know, you'd be so striking if you'd just—"

"No, nope." I cut her off. "We're not playing Dolly Dress-up. We're here to steal a dog, to sell that dog, and be on our way."

"Bits..." Bristol turns her big innocent eyes for appeal.

"No thanks," Bits says, either meaning she doesn't want to dress up either or she isn't gonna help, I can't tell, but it works for both.

"We never do what I want to do."

"We're doing what you want to do right now? And we did with the diamonds job? You act like we're always against you, it's kinda weird."

"Yes, but you're always on about *equipment* and plans of action and it just does get tiresome, darlings, I'm sorry."

"Real talk with Bristol at two o'clock in the afternoon," Bits says dryly.

"Hey, you wanna do solo work, you can. Nobody's saying we can't have side projects."

"Oh, I know, but I do like working with you girls. I was just hoping for some teambuilding."

"Maybe next time," I say, still grinning. "There's always bungee jumping, why don't we do that?" We all laugh, and it clears the air. But could it be possible that Bristol is lonely? That'd be wild. Maybe her Dubai friend group was having some kind of drama that she got impatient with. Maybe the real heist is the friends we made along the way.

Chapter Seven

The night before the auction, Bristol's out partying with new friends or acquaintances or connections, it's hard to tell which or maybe to her it's all the same, and me and Bits go to the convention center or whatever it's called where the auction'll be. It isn't the convention center with the bungee jumping anyway. The only auctions I've ever been to before were at barns and stuff, what do I know. I stopped at 7-Eleven again, bought all the hot dogs that they had on the rollers, and cut 'em up with a combat knife in the back of a van that we rented for a couple of hours. Well, that Bits rigged the system to think that we rented, for a couple of hours.

"One of the guards is out tonight," she says as we drive over, lying on the floor in the back with her headset on. "So they added to the drone patrols."

"Good news."

"Yup. I rerouted them a little last night, to see if it would work and if anybody would notice. It did, and they didn't."

"Double good news," I say. See, I have the active camo, but it's not gonna extend to the dog. "So you figure the middleman guy is actually French or is that just a language they had in common?"

"Hard to say. It's possible. And with people who're rich enough to pay millions of dollars for one single individual dog, well, rich people get weird. They could be from anywhere."

"Literally anywhere." I wonder if she's thinking about tigers. I'm thinking about tigers. "Good thing we're not that kind of rich people, right?"

"Is it weird that I don't think of myself as a rich people?"

I'd turn around to look at her for a sec, but with the headset on, Bitsy's facial expression isn't gonna mean anything. "No, I guess I don't either. I don't really do different things." Other'n drop off money to family members. Other'n have the money for fancyass prosthetics and to see a doctor once in awhile to make sure all the enhancers the army gave me are working right. Which they are. And especially after we deprogrammed all that goddamn posthypnotic shit, I've been feeling fine. I typically feel fine; it's what made me such a fit for the program to begin with. "Not expensive-pet-buying things." The robot dog doesn't count; something me and Bits could slap together an approximation of doesn't count as a weirdo rich person thing.

There's a long pause and then Bits says "Yeah true." Of course, she built that bleeding edge VR rig that she let me beat apart with a hammer, that was kinda the rich people thing to do. The one she slapped together at the Dubai house isn't nearly as involved, but she isn't spending her time totally conked out either, so I guess it's different. "We don't have cheetahs on gold leashes."

I park next to the building, do a quick equipment check, and hop out. "Catch you on the flip side," I say, and Bits laughs quietly in my earbud.

"Roger that," she says. "Did you bring enough hotdogs?"

"If I run out, we got bigger problems than explaining to Bristol that we tried to steal a march on her."

The truck locks behind me as I go to the door and swipe her fake keycard. I don't know what she did to make it work, if she snuck out here a different day or what, but it goes green and the lock clicks and I walk into a blank hall and flip on the camo. Why are the back ends of these places always so goddamn boring? Money sure but is that the only reason. I've got the map in my head and it's just a couple hallways before I'm at the dog room. I hear a drone at one point, but around a corner, and I trust Bits to nudge it away from me, if necessary. It's fine right now, anyway. What I also need is Bristol on the map in my head, so I know what *she's* up to, but the chances of us seeing her before we're all back at the hotel are slim. Also I just like knowing where people are. That's the rough thing about doing what I do and not being home anymore.

I swipe my fake keycard here and it buzzes but the door doesn't open. The light's yellow. "So hey..." I mutter.

"They've got another layer of security there hold on," Bits says. The numbers on the keypad start to light up like somebody's pressing them. I pucker my lips to whistle while I wait, stop myself. It's too quiet here for that. Probably nobody else whistles while they're on security detail. Plus I don't want to get the dogs riled up; it's shadowy in the room, but I can see at least one dog head in profile in a cage, and some eyes reflected in the hall light. I hope to christ they don't go nuts once I get in the room, or if they do, that any other human personnel just ignore it because dogs just bark sometimes, right. Or maybe they don't have the code to come in here, just the handlers do, so there's no point.

Oh, the handlers.

The door goes green and I open it, and I have the gun in my hand and that surge of adrenaline where I expect the room to have people in it to handle, but nobody's in here. I don't want to shoot somebody so I can steal a dog, so I'm glad, and Bits and Bristol have the tasers. Not that taze or shoot are my only options, obviously. There are any number of varyingly terrible things that I can do to a fellow human being, when called upon. But again, for a dog? Sure it's for a payday but. We were having those in Dubai, and nearly legit. Okay some companies would sue the shit out of us but that's neither here nor there.

I turn off the camo but don't turn the light on and the dogs have all stood up, judging from where their eye glows are, but aren't making any noise yet. Wait, no, one of them is growling way deep in their throat and if I had animal sense I'd've noticed it before now. "Relax, bud," I say quietly, and get out a handful of cut-up hotdog that I toss at each of the cages. Kennels? They aren't right next to each other, and there's collapsible room dividers between them. The dogs pay attention to the hot dogs while I look for a leash, and a collar, and the female.

The cages have little AR labels on 'em, so it's easy to figure it out. Both of the males are black with tan eyebrows, like a hound dog, but that's really the only hound dog similarity. Well maybe earset a little, but all three dogs have big fuckin' heads like lions. The female is the smallest; probably maybe half grown I guess. She's kind of a reddish golden color, like when retrievers get darker, and when I get close I can see the broad leather collar that she's wearing, part hidden by her fur. She looks at me suspiciously, and I toss her some more hot dog as I look at the kit nearby her. A leash, some grooming stuff, in a duffle. I pull out the leash, let it jingle a little. "Hey puppy girl, wanna go for a walk?" She looks at me when I talk, still chewing, but doesn't do anything else. Probably doesn't speak English, but that's fine, we'll figure it out. She isn't the one growling, anyway, that's one of the males. Both of the males. Growling in stereo. We're cool, it's good.

I hold out some hot dog to the bars of the cage and she sniffs at it audibly, then licks them out of my hand and ducks her head to pick it up. Okay good. I undo the top latch of the cage door, unlatch the bottom, and swing it open with a little creak. Her head comes up but she doesn't move. I think about reaching into the cage for her collar, think better of it, step back and crouch down. "C'mere. I got lots more hot dog where that came from."

She takes a step towards me, head tilted one way, and I drop hot dog right at my feet. She comes out of the cage readily, and I find her collar, rotate it around to clip the leash on the ring. She must be trained for handling, at least a little, so this is okay. She looks up at me after the leash clips, and I get more hot dog out of my pocket for her, and then grab her little travel bag. Might as well; she's gonna be at least overnight at the hotel with the new plan. I look in the cage to see if there's a toy or anything there but no, just a hamster bottle of water clipped to the side. Kind of weird, don't puppies chew? Whatever. Bits hasn't said anything yet but she's letting me hear her breathe which means she's getting impatient.

"How's it looking, Bitsy?" I ask, and again, the dog looks at me while I'm talking.

"Still okay for now. They have people doing the auction setup in the big facility so there's more people here than when we scouted."

"But they aren't back here, it's fine."

"You've got the dog right?"

"Yeah, comin' out now. Keep our exit clear."

"I will." She's laughing at me, probably. But it's always at this point of a job that I try not to think of everything that could go wrong and just work on the exit. Nothing fancy, nothing flashy, nothing extra. Got the thing, get the thing out. Unless the thing doesn't wanna get out. I take a few steps and the leash goes taut, and the dog is still standing there looking at me.

"Come on," I say, trying to make my voice inviting, not impatient. I could carry her, there's lots I could carry, I just don't want my face gettin' bit off. Please no prosthetic replacement face. Though could you get modular ones, so you could switch 'em out? What a tool that would be, in our life of crime. She tilts her head and looks at me the other way. Do I know some-thing in French that might get her moving? "Allez." Her dropped ears move a little, but I guess not. "Hey Bitsy, can you look up dog commands in Chinese for me?"

"What?"

"Nevermind." I get out more hotdog. Honestly, I don't want to feed this dog five pounds of hotdog and have her puke in the hotel and/or van but I also can't fuck around here for much longer. The hotdog works, the puppy follows along with me gently and happily as I manage the leash, the bag, and the hot-dog pieces. I wonder how dog people do it, it reminds me of seeing people somehow wrangle toddlers and toddler equip-ment. Everything is still weirdly quiet and I realize that she doesn't have any tags on her collar, and wonder what all those tags are, anyway. In case a dog gets lost, I guess, so they can get found. But that's what microchips are for anyway. Ooh, I hope Bits has a microchip reader. "Bits, you got a microchip reader?"

"Can you just shut up and get out here please?"

"Just askin'," I mutter. I consult the map in my head and reverse the turns I took coming in and then we're at the exit door, the dog and me, buddies now and requiring less hot dog. I let the door close quietly and let the dog sample the air with her snif-fer before I open the back of the van. Bits is sitting up now, VR headset hanging around her neck. "Okay, get in," I say to the dog, helpfully, as though she'll just hop up on cue. She looks up at me, looks at Bits in the van, looks up at me, and backs up a couple of steps. "Aw c'mon, here's more hot dog." I give her some, toss some in the van. Chewing, she considers it, paces back and forth a little as the leash allows. I wait. Bits inhales to say something and I shake my head. The dog gathers herself and hops up, snuffling around for the other hot dog pieces.

"Give me the leash," Bits says, and I toss the loop to her, put the bag down, shut the door.

"Hotel first and I'll return the van?"

"You'll...help me get her upstairs, right?"

"'Course I will."

"Yeah, then."

"Bristol still partying?" I roll us towards the road in neutral, keeping an eye in the rearview. Nothing going on. I start the van, turn on the lights, and a couple of blocks later we fade into traffic.

"Bristol's still partying," she says. So far so good.

Chapter Eight

The problem with stealing an auction item the night before the auction is set to go is they find out. I mean, they were obviously always gonna find out, but this many hours before the covert handoff, the police and other interested parties have that much more time to organize their searching. Which does and doesn't matter to us. We're in a cushy enough room in a cushy enough hotel that nobody's gonna be doing a room to room search here. We don't need to go ramming around the city with the dog, gettin' ourselves caught. We just wait for the handoff time, go, get paid.

Of course, Bristol doesn't know yet. That we've got the dog. Who is happy to cuddle in with me and sleeps nice the whole time. Exactly the kind of companionship you want a dog for. She wakes me up whining and then I realize the flaw in the plan, that dogs, unlike robot dogs, have to put the hot dogs somewhere when they're done with them.

"Wait a sec," I say, and the dog stops whining. She's probably gonna pee the bed, at the very least. Maybe not. This might've been easier with a boy dog. I go out into the common room of the suite and wander around. Quickly. There's some big baskets arranged as decoration, and have some moss looking stuff in them. Good enough? Maybe? I haul it to my room and put it in the corner, the dog sniffing intently as I do. I kind of point at it once it's settled and she looks at it looks at me, and starts circling. Rad. I leave her to do her business.

"My, you're up early," Bristol says when I come through the door between the suites and close it behind me. She's wearing one of the complimentary bathrobes. Oh I should message Bits that the dog is...doing her business.

"So're you, you were out late." She has fancy waters that she bought at some point, and is pouring one over ice. Has she been back long enough to sleep? Her and Bits, I swear, sometimes they really don't seem to get the value of some shuteye. You'd think Bristol would love her beauty sleep, and I guess she does, until something else has her attention. At least she isn't one of those party girls who also gets coked up, or maybe she does, but not enough that you can tell by the time she gets home. But I don't think she's like that, I don't think she'd ever let herself lose control like that. I know I don't really understand who'd want to; drinking, fine, smoking, sure of course, but there's a line. Everybody's got a line.

"I was making connections," she says airily. "The girls I met are friends with some local politicos, it would seem. There's quite the scene here."

"Oh, politicos," I say, like that means anything to me. Politicos are just lookin' to fuck people in order to get ahead. Not like, literally. Though also I guess sometimes literally. It's like venture capitalists. "I guess they probably got a scene everywhere, though, huh."

"Well yes. Though different scenes." She sips some of her water, then cocks her head, frowning just a little. "Do you hear that?"

I assume any 'that' is gonna be the puppy and listen accordingly but actually no, I don't hear her. I go over to the fancy 'sunken lounge' area and Bits is sprawled on the couch, but she's got a...well it's some kind of computery thing that's not a phone, that's buzzing like a phone would if it was on vibrate. "Oh that's where she is."

"You didn't know she wasn't in your room?"

I shrug, go poke at the coffee maker. "Well I didn't check."

Bristol gives a little laugh. "Darling, your beds are right next to each other."

"Yeah that's kinda weird for a swanky suite deal, ain't it?" I think the machine's brewing. Bits' little tech thing is still makin' noise and I go and kick the couch leg. I know better'n to put hands on somebody to wake 'em up. "Hey, is that important?"

She inhales sharply, gives a little jerk, and paws the VR thing up off her eyes and I watch her pupils contract in the light. She blinks at me for a sec before feeling around, putting the buzzing right in front of her face. It's got a metal casing. "Oh."

"Oh, what?" Bristol asks, in a too-casual tone. I dunno if right now's when she caught on we were up to something, or if it's just when she decided let us know she knew we were up to something. Always hard to tell with her, she's got a helluva a poker face. The best bluffer I've ever known.

"Well I wrote some code that would route through a vpn that I don't use all the time and ping through...well okay that doesn't matter, but if a certain thing happens it sets off an alarm in this." She shakes the little box, as though we have any fuckin' idea what it is. "So that it wouldn't be traceable to any of the equipment I typically have up and running."

"Well okay what happened?"

She sits up, stretching, and the coffeemaker does a sputtering steaming thing that seems to suggest it's done. It smells done. I go and take out two cups, look at Bristol, who nods, take out a third. Let's see, Bits like sweet and black, Bristol likes pale and sweet, and I'll drink it any old way so I just leave mine black. Bristol probably also likes balloon animals or something made out of the foam but I'm not making foam.

The thing isn't vibrating anymore when I hand Bits her coffee.

"Okay, so—" she says and Bristol's phone rings.

Bristol looks at it, I assume to cancel the call, and then her eyebrows go up and she answers it, pacing away. The person on the other end is talking even as she gets it to her ear. Nope, I still don't speak French. Spanish, yeah. Maybe I should get like, those recordings you play when you sleep, or whatever, learn it subliminally. Couple of our buddies back home, they learned French to sign up for the French Foreign Legion, god knows where they even heard of it. Operator messenger boards or some shit. God knows why the French Foreign Legion is even still a thing, and why it accepts people who aren't French.

Bits looks at me and I shrug. "I assume the two are linked," I say dryly.

"Yeah," she says, then she lowers her voice. "The dog?"

"I brought her a plant so she could do her thing." Bits blinks and kind of frowns a little, but then Bristol comes back.

"Well, everything's ruined," she says cheerfully, taking a sip of her coffee and then setting it down. "Somebody stole the dog last night, the auction is off, and my contact is *freaking* out. I've never heard him like that before, ever. Just inconsolable, the poor dear, this really is more than he can bear."

"I thought he was an intermediary?" Bits says.

"Well excuse me for not having a map of their organization, being an intermediary doesn't mean it isn't still important to him, evidently."

"Organization?" Maybe we should've asked her more to begin with. Not that it matters much. We don't need to know why the dog, we just had to get dog from point A to Person B. Which we can still do.

She wave a hand, picks up her coffee again. "I don't know that there's an *organization*, I was just using it as an exaggeration. Family tree? Is that better?"

"Yeah, sure." I shrug. "But anyway, Bits?"

"Well I had this set for—"

"Bits, I'm dreadfully sorry, but now isn't really the time to talk about your gadgets, we need to find out where the dog is, and who took her, and why they knew that she's the one that was—"

In the adjoining suite, the dog must've finished her business, and we'll see how that went, or maybe she was just bored of hearing people's voices and not being able to see anybody. I should've left food out for her, there was food in that bag. But she barks and it is loud. Bristol stops midsentence, midgesture, and blinks slowly. Wets her lips. Takes a breath and gives her head a little shake. Looks at me.

"Dolly, what was that?"

"Oh that? It was—" I'm tryin' real hard not to laugh at the look on her face.

"Did you two steal the dog already? Is the dog in your suite?" Pretty soon her voice is gonna be a tone that only the dog can hear.

"Surprise?" Bits says hopefully and I can't help it anymore, I just laugh. I set down my coffee so I don't spill it.

"When did you...*why* did you?"

"Last night, and we were bored while you were at a party so we figured we'd just go scoop her up." I go to the door between suites and open it. The dog is standing there and swishes her tail a little when she sees me, but her head is down. "You hungry? Let me get a bowl for your food."

"You were bored," Bristol says faintly, and sits in one of the plush armchairs.

"Well we hoped it'd be a nicer surprise but the cat's out of the bag. Or the dog is out of the. Bag." That saying doesn't really work with a not-baggable animal. I get a bowl from the kitchenette and bring it over to the dog, who's still standing between the rooms. "I gotta get past you for your food."

"Oh but that's what the code was about, when people were sending out the alarm about the dog, so I can make sure it isn't tracking to us. And nothing is," Bits says helpfully.

"Delightful, I'm sure," Bristol says, still very quiet, looking at the dog. "I suppose I should call—"

"Yeah go call Pierre or whoever back and let him know he can stop losing his shit. Everything's fine." The dog hasn't moved. "Hey come on." She blinks up at me, and then backs up all the way into the room, then turns her head and yawns. "Let's see what they've got for you. Some kinda meat cereal I'm sure."

I wasn't sure Bristol could hear me, but she sighed elaborately, then paused, and then was speaking French again. Good. No need for the hullaballoo. Though I guess now whoever her guy is is gonna have to figure out how to act natural until we can meet up with him and do the handoff. There are little containers of varying things, but I'm looking for simple, and there is kibble that I pour into the bowl. The dog sniffs it, then looks up without moving her head and growls. You'd think, with all that fur, it'd be too heavy to see any of it stand up, but she manages.

I look where she's looking and Bits is standing in the doorway. "So I guess she's nervous?"

"Prob'ly definitely nervous. You got any idea yet why Bristol's buddy might want her? You figure she's got a microchip with CIA intel on it or something? Chinese government? Russia again?"

"I guess we'll find out when we scan her for a chip. Or chips. Not while she's eating though." Bits sits on the edge of her bed. The dog yawns again, and then she does start crunching her kibble. I wonder how much I should've given her.

"Yeah definitely not." I look through the doors, at Bristol with her phone smile on, soothing nerves and rerouting plans like a champ. "Well that went okay."

"It could've been a lot worse." Bits smiles a little, looking at something else. Or maybe not. Her mind is always on other things. "I assume we'll still do the handoff tonight."

"Yeah, don't see why not." I look through the door into Bristol's suite, where she's sitting again, still on the phone, and seems much more relaxed now. "Seems like things're smoothed over."

"I think so?" She shrugs.

The dog finishes eating and stares at me again. "Oh, water." I fill up the bowl in the bathroom sink, put it down for her, and she laps it up noisily.

Bristol comes to the doorway, still in her robe, now with her coffee. "Well I'm still going to the auction, because at this point it would look odd if I didn't."

"Plus you don't wanna waste the new dress."

"Plus that," she agrees, that sharp little edge in her voice that we get when she means business. "It's possible I'll make other useful connections there."

"Or see something else you like," Bits points out helpfully.

"Perhaps." So she doesn't expect that at all. I didn't look at the catalogue, really, I dunno what else is gonna be on the auction block.

"Gonna wear your special shoes?"

"Oh, no, they're for Paris next month." And she shuts the door and goes to change.

Chapter Nine

O f course we go as backup when Bristol goes to the auction. The windows of the car that she for-real rents are tinted enough that it doesn't matter I'm not dressed like a chauffer, and the back is spacious enough that it doesn't matter that Bits is sprawled in the footwells with her head in VR. She's got all the cameras before we're on site and feeds Bristol information about who's already arrived, about security, about media, because there is media. "This is gonna flag you, you realize," Bits says.

Bristol smiles a smile that only I can see, and says "Oh yes, darling, I'm well aware." Our eyes meet in the rearview and she winks at me. I got no clue what level of 3D social chess she's playin' and I'd just as soon be left out of that aspect of the festivities, please. I like things to be more direct, which again, isn't to say I'm in a real hurry to use this nice handgun I got. And while I've got a couple fast escape-from-Macau notions in my head, none of 'em involve also having a dog that isn't ours. Let's hope it won't come to that.

She gets out in the snowstorm of camera flashes and strides confidently up the walkway. I guess celebrities are expected to be at this gig, and I wonder who the photographers assume she is. Somebody's girlfriend or mistress probably. Somebody's go-between. They've latched onto her, fascinated by the mystery, and of course she fucking loves that. I watch for a sec, then drive away before the car behind us honks.

"I've got a stopwatch running on the first agency sort of communication I notice," Bits says from behind me.

"I expect nothing less." I think about making a bet, stop myself. No good borrowing trouble, no matter how fun it might be. Not like I'm very fucking cautious in my overall living. "Y'know, she mentioned that she had makeup that—"

"Messed with the cameras? Yeah that's the pictures that people are posting on local groups, it's like she's got a mask of light." Bits puts one of the images in the car's dashboard screen for a second, for me to see.

"Modern problems require modern solutions," I say dryly, fish the ecigarette out of my jacket pocket. I actually like real cigarettes better, it's weird to go around smelling like cookies and cinnamon rolls and stuff in my particular area of expertise. It's...the word isn't contradictory, Bristol would know the word. It's like naming your big dangerous killer 'Bubbles.' Or I guess like having your normal-sized dangerous killer named Dolly, so really I'm just provin' my own point. At least I don't have to figure out what to do with the cigarette butts, if I'm using an ecig. You'd think they would've come up with a better kind by now. Biodegradable. Eco-friendly. Edible. "You don't mind?" I ask, not thinking about how she can't see me, won't know what I'm talking about.

"It's okay." Okay, fair enough.

Macau's a nice place to drive around in, actually, especially at night if you get away from the main traffic. There's a good loop you can do that still keeps you close to where you need to be. In case you need to swoop in and give somebody a fast getaway. Or have a deep and sudden need for luxury goods shopping in an indoor mall that has gondolas and a painted sky. I cruise, keeping an eye on the vehicle's charge, wonder what I'd do to make money if I lived here. Could join one of those rideshare companies. Could do security for a club, or even one of the hotels, though I'm probably not polished enough in my appearance, in a manner of speaking. I haven't noticed a single mechanic's, but that doesn't mean they ain't here.

I think about the dog, but we put her in one of the bathrooms with food and water and a blanket from one of the beds, or a duvet Bristol called it. I don't know what the fuckin difference is between a duvet and a comforter and a bedspread, but I guess there is one.

"How's it looking?" I ask after awhile. Place like this, you don't want the camera watchers watching you pass by too many times. Switching the route too much would take me too far away, but I don't want to be noticeably parking either. "How long's this shindig supposed to take?"

"They're almost to the dogs now, and they definitely didn't say that the dog's been stolen or missing or anything, just that she's no longer being auctioned tonight. Somebody left right after that and made a call, it bounced off a local tower. Bristol didn't comment on it, so it's fine, or she didn't know who they were. The paparazzi didn't say anything about them either." A long pause, but normal in Bitsy's way of doing things. "Okay that person went back to the auction."

"Okay." She puts him on the screen for me, a kind of sandy-haired white guy, maybe in a black suit or maybe it's a tux, who cares. Nobody I recognize, so that's good. "Send that to Bristol too."

"Already did."

"So what's the demographic of our buyers here?"

"Are you asking if he and Bristol are the only white people? They aren't."

"You really know how to put somebody at ease." I grin, take a different loop this time. Maybe I should learn how to blow smoke rings, that'd work for both real cigarettes and the e ones. Nothing too fancy, just a good old fashioned ring. I hope the dog is sleeping.

"It's what you wanted to know!"

"Naw, it is. Did she say anything when you sent it."

"No, but that could mean anything. She knows him, she's never seen him before in her life, they used to go out…"

"That's our girl." No telling how many notches Bristol has on her belt, or even what a notch on her belt means to her. Just a few dates or actually lettin' him run the bases. When the topic comes up she just kinda smiles mysteriously and says that a lady never tells, or something. Bits just always kinda shrugs, so I'm guessing she's never felt particularly inspired on the topic, and pretty much neither of 'em are interested in my range of conquests, from one of my closest road crew friends back home to a stewardess that one time in Berlin. Maybe those things are best kept quiet, who am I to say. It's kind of a pity the stewardess thing didn't work out, but she was too nervous about things, and I wouldn't've been able to be honest with her, and that's just no way to have a relationship.

"Looks like there are other cars pulling up," Bits says. "I don't know if it's a problem yet."

"Pulling up out front or out back?"

"Out back."

"That weren't there before?" I'm already turning around to take the direct route back to the conference center.

"I'm running their plates against the data I pulled before...no. They weren't there before."

"I don't suppose what they're packing is also wifi enabled."

She starts to say something, probably tell me that's not what it's really called, and I know that's not what it's really called. Then she says "I didn't scan for that, but I can see them on the cameras and it mostly looks like holstered handguns. They're in suits or street clothes and filtering into the building, this isn't geared paramilitary."

"Fair enough." The paparazzi have mostly cleared away when I pull back up. "Tell milady her chariot is here."

"I already did."

I tap my fingers on the steering wheel. "Soooo..."

"Give her a minute. Nothing's wrong yet inside, she doesn't want to Cinderella, she said."

"What, is she talkin' to a literal prince who might take her away from all this?"

"I am not going to ask her that," she sighs.

I laugh. "Surprised you don't already know."

"I don't background check everybody that walks past us." She sounds a little huffy but more distracted than anything else.

"Guess it would get tiring." Still no Bristol. I'm not the only car here at least, and I don't see anybody looking our way, not from the conference center side of things or from the across the street way of things.

"Yeah. And it's mostly boring. So many people are just really boring."

"Not like us."

"Mmmm." She's real quiet back there. It's amazing to me, how just effortlessly still she can be, and for how long she can do it. I can do it, but it takes a lot of concentration. And it's exhausting, the effort of doin' nothing. Or, doing nothing in anticipation of sudden and vigorous activities, typically of the violent sort. Maybe also with some running and lifting. Climbing, stairs or fences. "Here she comes."

"Thank Christ." We were none of us raised religious, but still. I adjust my rearview so I can see that front walkway, and when I finally see Bristol, I can't hear her, but in my head I can hear the sharp clack clack that her heels're making, at that pace. She's still moving too slow for my comfort, and stops for a painful thirty seconds to talk to one of the paparazzi, her head tilted just a little, nodding, laughing. "Tell her to—"

"I already did."

Then finally, finally, she's sliding into the back seat and I'm pullin' away about the second she's got the door closed, maybe a half tic earlier than that but who's counting. There's nothing guaranteeing there's gonna be gunplay inside, or that the people attending the auction even know that there's a whole buncha guys with guns cruising the halls that I cruised last night, but there's nothing guaranteeing that won't go sour, and we want to be well clear of that. We're all well familiar with brushin' up against the law, and it doesn't make it any sweeter with repetition.

"Y'know, we spend an awful lotta time drivin' you away from situations," I say.

"In a very large way, you caused this situation," she says, smirking.

"You didn't still have to come to the auction," Bits says, still on the floor.

"Oh but I did, it is always such a learning experience, rubbing elbows with these types."

"I'm sure," I say. I'd ask Bits if anybody noticed us or is follow-ing us, but that's why she's still on the floor. Just gotta trust the process. Bitsy knows what she's about. Honestly, we're lookin' pretty good right now. "Anything you want to share with the rest of the class?"

"From the auction? I don't imagine there was anything you were interested in, no." I glance at her in the rearview, and she does seem to be genuinely considering. "I did receive anoth-er message from our intermediary, just confirming our engage-ment this evening."

"Again?" That was just this morning that they hashed every-thing out again.

"He *is* rather nervous."

"Apparently. Not really so great for him, to be in business like this."

"I get the sense it isn't his usual."

I let that ride for a little while, counting the streetlights. "Get the sense? I thought you two were old friends." Wait a second, Bristol treats everybody she meets like old friends.

She does one of those light little laughs, that make you think about blowing bubbles on a summer afternoon when you were a kid and you didn't have to do much decision making. "Oh heavens no, I first spoke to him about six months ago I'd say."

"Have you been...planning this for six months."

"No, the day he asked me about it was the day I told you girls about it. My friend in Tokyo might know him better; she thought well enough of him to refer me for the job."

"Alright then." Six more streetlights. "But he knew about us?"

"Of *course* not, not specifically. He knew that I had associates."

"And so does your Tokyo associate."

"Oh yes, she does. *You* remember meeting her that once, when we were all in London? Keiko?"

"At that Oxford party." Okay, yeah, I did remember Bristol's Keiko. Doesn't pay to second guess Bristol, but she leaves a hell of a lot out more than Bits does. "Okay, so we swing by the hotel for the dog, then we rendezvous and then, what, numbered bank account? Briefcase of cashola? Cryptocurrency?" I'm not second guessing. I'm just starting to feel real weird about this. Maybe not starting. Starting to acknowledge that I feel weird about this.

"Half numbered bank account, half cash." She's checking her makeup in a little mirror she pulled out of her little purse. "And anyway, Bits already has the bank account information."

"Yup. And already disseminated the funds."

"Oh, fair enough." I guess that says a lot about who I am as a person, that I haven't noticed a big ol' deposit into my bank account. Well. My business bank account.

"I don't imagine he'll be so gauche as to put it in a briefcase."

"No of course not," I say, thinking of the briefcases of diamonds we once emptied. "Nobody ever does anything like that."

Chapter Ten

There's still a ton of people milling in and out of the Venetian for the shopping experience, so it isn't super late. I park as close to an entrance as I can manage and saunter in, leaving Bits and Bristol to hash out who's gonna sit in the front and who's gonna sit with the dog. I've got my guesses about how that arrangement'll shake out, but I'll just have to wait and see. I make it up to the room and get the bathroom door open before Bits is in my earpiece. The dog actually seems kind of happy to see me, she isn't lifting her lip or anything. Lookin' at me sideways with all the whites of her eyes showing. I crouch down and she comes to me, slowly, and when I hold my hand out she sniffs it and then bumps it with her nose.

"The contact just called in a panic, we gotta go."

"Without the dog, I assume?"

"Yeah, leave her for now."

"Roger that." I give her a quick pat and say "Sorry, pup, I'll try to be right back," and I'm out the door again, making sure the do not disturbs are still up. They are, and there's another tag hung so that we can indicate when we do want service. I'll let Bristol handle that when we get back. "Bristol is this guy always so flighty?"

"No, actually, this has been an exceedingly odd situation."

"In the six months that you've known him."

"Yes, in the six months that I've known him," she snaps. "Please don't *harp*, it isn't as though it will help a single thing."

"Sorry." Not sorry but. Sometimes you gotta pay lipservice to peacekeeping, not technically a lie. I get outside and get back in the car. "Okay where to?"

"I put his location in the car's GPS," Bits says. She's still in the back seat, headset around her neck, and Bristol is up front, so I would've won money on that bet.

"You know, this might be the first time we're ever like. To the rescue."

"I think it is."

"Oh please don't call it that, darlings." I cut my eyes to Bristol, and while she isn't exactly wringing her hands, she's tense.

"If there's something else goin' on here, now might be a good time to fill us in," I say.

"I told you the entire story, cross my heart. My contact was paid to reach out to us to get the dog for his employers. Beyond the price these dogs go for, I don't know what makes the one we've dognapped special, and I *certainly* didn't know that other parties were interested as well."

"I feel like we gotta start making a mental note that other parties're gonna be interested. Just add it to the mission checklist."

"Yes that's all well and good but—"

"Bristol, cool it. We'll get your guy, he'll get the dog, we go our separate ways. Everything's copacetic. We don't need to know what's up with the dog, that's not what we're getting paid for."

"Looks like we'll be there in five," Bits says.

"Oh good," Bristol says, shifting in her seat, resting her hand lightly on the door handle. She's ready to roll out, which is great. Whatever you might think about Bristol at first or even second glance, there's always more to her. I haven't seen her actually have to hit somebody more than a couple of times, but she's definitely got a crafted capability. I wonder if she learned that in her little online classes too. Old videos. Some kind of combat yoga spa retreat.

I look at the GPS in the dashboard, at our little blip getting closer and closer to his little blip, and I've got the feeling that we won't be in time for...whatever this is. I still try, within reason, even pushing reason, trusting Bitsy to have an eye on things like radar and police and all that. It's late enough that there is and isn't traffic, are and aren't pedestrians, and I make the final turn sharply enough that all of the tires are gently singing, like if you run a wet finger along a glass rim. I hear Bits' teeth clack together when I stop and we all slam out of the vehicle and I've gotta hand it to Bristol, she actually can haul ass in high heels. It's a public garden or a park or something, and we go through a stone arch, and then up a whole bunch of stairs, and then we see him on a walkway, leaning on a railing, looking out across the little lake there. Reservoir, inlet, whatever.

And at first I think I was wrong. Just 'cause I go with my gut a whole lot doesn't mean I like being right about bad stuff. There aren't any lights up here, just some globe lamps in the park below, and the glow from the city. It isn't ideal but I let Bristol get to him first, he's her contact and he's already spooked, right? She gets to him and he doesn't react and I'm right behind her and she touches his shoulder and he's not leaning on the railing he's draped on the railing and starts to go over but I shove past her and grab a handful of his wet suitcoat and haul him back. He kathumps on the pavement the way no conscious person can and I was still holdin' out for unconscious but then I look at my hand and of course it's blood.

Bristol puts her hand to her mouth like she's shocked, just shocked, and maybe she is. It's just so quiet, even with the city all around us. Not even birds. Bits gets in there, though, kneels down and pulls his phone out of his inside coat pocket, blinks at it. "Can you turn him over? He's got something else, I think in a pants pocket." I oblige, and she pulls out a flat data pack or maybe another phone, it's not a gun so my expertise is limited. She pulls his wallet too.

Bristol walks past a few steps, as though maybe whoever did this is at the other end of the walkway just waiting and watching, but I can't see anybody, and if Bits picked up any electronics over there, she'd've already let us know. The internet of things makes it real hard to be sneaky sometimes. But if I was gonna shoot somebody here, I'd have my team spook them so they'd come out on this bridge and I'd drop 'em without them feeling a thing. Oh shit. Oh we are so fucking stupid.

"We need to get outta here," I say, but there's no time, all the hairs on the back of my neck standing up a split second before I tackle Bristol over the railing, hearing the rifle crack once, then again, feel the wind of a round right by my face and the white-hot sear of one creasing the side of my neck, but by the third crack we've plunged into the water.

I don't know if Bristol can swim. I assume she can. For me, growin' up, there were all kinds of lakes and things by us. And we had that stereotypical Southern Gothic swimming hole that all the kids went to. Rope swing, ancient tree, kids driving out there to neck, the whole nine. Shallow by the shore, with weeds and stuff that people would pull up periodically so you can wade in without gettin' all wrapped up, but it got real deep in the middle. No idea how deep, I'm sure there's records some-where, but not that we had access to. But once, I jumped off the rope swing with a belt that I tied a buncha crap to, so I'd get to the bottom right quick. Just wanted to prove I could do it.

Grabbed a handful of silt and rocks there with my left hand, while I undid the belt with my right hand. Pretty much blacked out on the way back up. My oldest brother pulled me out, curs-ing a blue streak, and the last thing I remember before actually blacking out is looking up at our friend Butler and shoving my balled up fist of silt and rocks and stuff at him until he held his hands out. Then I opened my hand and let go. And then I let go. Might be the first time I ever blacked out, actually. Some-thin' to put in the baby book. There was a super old coin in that wad of stuff, and he had it made into a belt buckle that I wore until I lost it, and there was a cowboy spur, and I had that made into a belt buckle he wears. I assume he still wears. I'm not sayin' he's carrying a torch but...

Anyway we don't hit bottom, and I keep a hand on Bristol as I swim off for where I think the right shore is, and where I hope cover is. I don't think my neck's too bad, just a graze, more on the meat than near anything vital. Stings like a bitch. I don't hear any more gunfire, and I have to trust that Bits'll keep her head down and get back to the car without getting aerated. Bristol seems to be doing okay, swimming, not dead weight that I'm dragging. I don't think she's hit, I didn't feel her shudder on our way down. You don't forget what that shudder's like. I'm not gonna forget what that shudder's like, not for all of my days. I hope Bits isn't hit. I gotta think about what the plan is, if one or both of 'em did get shot.

That first breath when I break the surface both burns and is sweet relief, and Bristol's trying not to sputter and cough but really needs to sputter and cough and I haul her up onto the shore where there's some bushes and stuff, and between that and the angle, that shooter shouldn't have a shot anymore. That shooter should've cleared out already, just discharging an un-suppressed rifle in a city like that at least three times. There's some distant sirens but honestly, when aren't there?

She finally gives in to the coughing, her face buried in her arms, and we lay there for awhile and catch our breath. She lost her shoes but not her purse, so I guess it's a good thing she didn't wear the fancy schmancy ones. "Bits?" I finally say, when things seem quiet.

"I'm at the car, I'm going to do a lap and then come back for you."

"Understood." I think we've got tree cover all the way back to the parking lot. We should probably even go further, up the road a little, before Bits stops. In case whoever that was is also doing a lap and coming back for us. "You okay?" I ask Bristol. Our earbuds and stuff, it all can work subvocally, if we bother to take that care. Right now, I'm botherin' to take that care.

"Yes," she says after a moment. Somebody could be standing a foot away and not hear us, other than our creep-on-the-phone breathing. "How did you—"

"Sometimes you just know," I say. Because while I can't explain my timing, I definitely understood the setup. There's honestly no good reason we aren't both dead or bleeding, unless the gunman was about done packin' it in when we arrived and had to set up again. But that's a weird decision to make. The world may never know. I got a bandanna in my pocket and hold it against my neck and I can see the flash of Bristol's eyes as she looks at me. Of course I'd get just a little bit shot where none of the gear covers.

We lay there awhile longer and then Bits says "Everything is clear, unless they've just gone dark."

"I guess we gotta take that chance," I say. Can't say why, but I'd lay money that they're gone, not hanging around waiting, not circling back go look for us. I'm laying our lives on it, I guess, and that's worth more than money. I squeeze out my bandana, figuring it's mostly the lake water, then twirl it and tie it around my neck. Not quite a right fit, but kinda on the right spot. "You ready Bristles?"

"I suppose," she says with a little sigh, pulling that carelessness around her like a shawl.

"Okay, I'll meet you just up the road from the parking lot," Bits says, and we sneak through the park until we get to path again. Wait. Look around. Then we keep going, cutting over where we probably shouldn't be walking until we get to the street, right as Bits pulls over onto the shoulder.

"Everything still clear?" I ask. Until today we've just sat around for awhile, but also the thought of breakin' down all my equipment and getting it dried out right when we get back to the hotel is exhausting. I'll ride it out, though, can't let stuff sit like that.

Bits shrugs. "Seems to be. None of the police even came through here."

"Makes sense."

"Does it?" Bristol asks from the back seat. She's leaned over, rolling off her stockings. I forget that she wears 'em, but she's also said they're protective in some way. Guess they must be, if they didn't shred right off her feet on our walk through the park.

"I'm not sure any of it does, but close enough."

"Do you want me to look at that?" She leans forward, but doesn't touch me.

"Nah, it's probably fine."

"Look at what?" Bits looks at me, then her eyes get big. "Dolly!"

"I'm okay, Jesus, look at the road won't you? Gotten worse than this slamming my hand in a door."

Chapter Eleven

—————

We park at the hotel and Bits does something to extend the rental and we walk through the quiet lobby to the elevator. I'm sure that overnight guy has seen a lot wilder than whatever picture we make. He just kind of fades back away from the desk to the offices they've got, and I think he's been the same guy every time, gotta remember to leave him a good tip. We get into the elevator and somehow, other than not having shoes, Bristol looks...fine? She's got some kinda personal grooming magic, I tell you what. I very definitely look like I jumped in a reservoir with all my clothes on and then tramped through the woods and maybe bled a little. I think it's stopped already, the papercut of bullet wounds I guess. Bits looks like Bits. Normally I don't concern myself with the way we as a group appear to others, I'm not sure it's the best time to start.

When we're in the elevator, I can't help but ask "So there wasn't anything else about the dog that you knew of? Data in the microchip? Did she swallow diamonds or something that somebody's gonna want?"

"No, nothing," Bristol says. "She's just a dog that's important to them, I don't know why. We may never know."

"I'm hoping that there's something worth it in his phone, or on this," Bits says. I realize that the other thing she got out of the guy's pocket was a hard drive or something. But a hard drive on its own doesn't throw a signal, even I know that. "And I macgyvered something to scan the dog's microchip, I just thought we'd be done by now."

"Oh good," Bristol sighs, and fishes in her soggy purse for her keycard. The lock beeps and when she pushes the door open, the dog barks. She sounds a little closer than Bits and my bathroom, though, and I swipe our keycard and go into our suite in a hurry. I remember opening our bathroom door, petting the dog, getting the call, leaving. Not closing the door.

"C'mere girl!" I say from our suite which looks pretty okay. A torn-up fast food bag on the ground, whatever, the garbage can doesn't have a lid on it. Oh and there's some couch fluff, that's a little less okay. Oh and the pillows have feathers in them, should've expected that I guess. Well. Had feathers.

"Dolly could you come in here, please?" Bristol calls through our open dividing door, tone strained almost to the pitch that only the dog could hear. Again.

"Sure thing." I look around, grab the dog's leash from the counter where I left it. The door to the hall is closed, Bits must be with Bristol. Or she went back out to the car and just drove away. I wouldn't blame her.

The pillows didn't survive in Bristol's room either. Or the comforter or duvet or whatever the fuck it is. The dog is in the little sunken living room thing, in the corner near the sliding glass door, and she'd got enough hair standing up that she looks maned, like a lion. Her ears are pinned and she's growling deep in her chest. Bristol's standing closer to her than I would've expected, holding something I can't really see. I come a little closer, note Bits by the mini bar.

There's red stuff on the floor, and around the dog's mouth, which is hard to see with all the fur. "Hold up, is that blood? Did she bite you? Did she hurt herself?"

"It isn't blood, it's....it's a LeBoutin."

Ohhh the shoes. "That sounds expensive."

"Because it *is*," Bristol says, a real snap to her voice.

"Look maybe come away from there, she's scared. The shoes're toast, I'm sorry, that's on me. I didn't close her in the bathroom again when you called me."

"Scared? She's ready to tear my leg off."

"Because you look like you want to hurt her, come on. We took her from anybody she knew, then left her alone in an unfamiliar place. She's a dog, not a person, it's not like she knows what being a guest is."

Bristol does back away from the dog, and turns towards me. I may never have seen her so angry, red spots burning high on her cheeks. I guess I understand now why people use blush. "Just because you've spent so much time with that *robot* doesn't mean you know anything about real dogs."

I don't know why that stings so much, why it matters, but I guess we're all just bundles of nerves right now. To my credit, I don't step any closer to her, but my hands go into fists just on their own. I've hit people for far less. "Look. I get that those shoes were special for you. I get that a guy you kinda knew died, and that's a terrible thing. And I know not a whole lot of people say this to you, Bristol, but please. Shut the fuck up."

Bits makes a noise like choking and maybe she's laughing. Maybe it is funny, and I'll laugh about it later. Maybe Bristol too. Right now, though, she looks shocked. "Dolly, I think it would be best if—"

"Yeah, I'm gonna go next door and cool down. Come on, pup." I whistle like I trained her, and the dog comes right to me, her steps slinking as she passes Bristol, getting more normal when she gets to my side. I go back between the doors and close them. I don't mean to separate Bits, she can do whatever. But Bristol and I need that separation. It isn't the first spat we've had, it'll be fine. But boy howdy does it not feel fine.

The thing about having a dog around you when you're pissed, is you try to feel un-pissed real quick. You don't want the dog to think they're the reason you're mad. They just don't get it. This dog isn't cringing, she's got a very 'yeah what?' attitude, but still. She came to me, that's something. I guess a thing to do first is get out my first aid kit, disinfect what I've got going. It looks awful in the mirror, immediately much better once I get the blood and leaves and lake gunk cleaned off me. Not even a thing worth trying to stitch, it looks more like a hot iron got laid against my skin for a sec. I kinda shake out the gun and leave it on the bathroom counter for now.

After awhile, Bits comes in, using the hallway door. The dog is following me around as I pick up garbage and put it in one of the pillowcases that's also fucked. I've been party to cleanup from military-type parties that got out of hand, one kinda busy dog doesn't really compare. No, not even comparing where she shit on the floor. Things just get outta hand sometimes.

"Are you okay?" she asks after watching me for a little while

"Yeah." What a weird question, and then I realize she probably means the injury, not my feelings. "Yeah, it's fine."

"We aren't normally like this," she says.

"I'd guess having a team mascot is right out," I say.

"At least the kind that eats shoes." She pops the tab on an energy drink.

"Am I wrong, that we can just get her another pair?"

"Nope. I even just reserved them at the store here. She doesn't know that yet."

"Then what's the problem?" I look at the room, twirling the pillowcase shut so I can knot it. Looking good, I think. Bits shrugs, her eyes in that slightly off to the side way. She's still enough that the dog eventually goes and sniffs around her, then gets on one of the couches, lying down but kinda stiffly, with her head up.

"I don't really know," Bits eventually says. "I couldn't find anything we should be worried about, like anybody from an agency coming for us. Social media of her friends back in Dubai seems fine, and nobody's blocked or unfriended or anything. She's texting a normal sort of amount, I think, and doesn't have any meetings set up or anything that was canceled."

I stare at her and then just laugh. "*Elizabits*! What were we just talking about?"

"I only do it when somebody's acting weird." She blinks and looks at me with kind of a frown. "And anyway, the guy that died tonight, she really did only meet him like six months ago. And they weren't dating or anything, that's not the kind of upset she is."

"Well, we do what we can to not leave a body count, maybe it's just that." Bristol's as stone cold as any of us, but in different ways. It's possible. Though also, I'm real curious about Bits's metric for whether somebody's bein' weird or not. She must have a program that runs, and compares our actions against our new habits. That's how I'd decide it, if I was like. Surveilling somebody.

"I'm not sure yet who he was working for and who was going to pay us, but I'm getting there. And then later, or maybe tomorrow, I'll see about her microchip. There was a number listed in the auction catalog. Have you looked at her collar and tags, do they seem normal?"

"I have not investigated that, no." The dog is looking between the two of us as we talk, not moving her head really, just sort of raising one eyebrow and then the other. Well, what would be eyebrows on a person. Is it eyebrows on a dog?

"Tomorrow," Bits says. "You look tired and I've got these other leads to chase."

"Bitsy are you sendin' me to bed?"

"Maybe." She smiles a little.

"Well I'm gonna hit the showers first, anyway. I guess holler if you need me." The dog watches me go, but doesn't follow me, and I take a shower that's first as hot as I can stand, and use all the smelly things the hotel provides, just to say I did, and then as cold as I can stand, just to round things out. I remember Bristol sayin' once that cold water closes the follicles of your hair or something and reduces frizz, I dunno. I don't really care about frizz so much, other than that static isn't good for the weirdly sensitive electronics that equipment sometimes has. Frizz has been a losing battle my whole life, so I gave up caring. Plus the cold feels good on my neck.

There's something botherin' me, I've got that tip-of-the-tongue feeling like when you're trying to think of a word, except it's my brain both trying to ask and answer a question that I'm not really informed on. Maybe it's just that I'm tired; we've gone awhile without this kind of action, which is a good thing, but you can't let things like that go too long if you wanna stay sharp.

Bits is reclined and in VR land when I come out of the bathroom, and the dog is lying on the floor between the beds.

When I lie down, I pat the bed for her to get up, and after a couple minutes, she does. She killed a couple of the pillows when we were gone, but good news, there's about a hundred of them, so it's not really a big deal.

Chapter Twelve

——

I wake up knowing exactly what's wrong, but no idea how to fix it. I roll over and Bits is still sleeping or still in VR, who can tell, but I lean way over to the other bed and shove the mattress a few times, until the frame creaks, hissing between my teeth at the stretch and pull of my new scab. "Bits, we fucked up."

"What?" She jerks bolt upright, pawing the goggles off her face. The dog raises her head and watches her. "What's wrong?"

"I know what's wrong with Bristol."

"Christ, Dolly, you scared me." She blinks at me, looks around the room, looks at the dog and then at me again. "Okay what."

"That time she spent with Homeland last year."

Bits blinks at me, slower this time. "Oh."

"Yeah. Yup." Bristol's all about maintaining outward appearances, but Jesus, we shouldn't've expected her to be okay after that. Or not so okay, so quickly. Maybe she's putting that expectation on herself too, I'd guess she probably is, but also I think I've got it exactly nailed, the weirdness, the tension.

"Okay but what do we...do?"

"Well I don't know. Clearly a puppy was not the right answer."
I grin and she laughs, and I stretch and get up. "I also feel kinda
awkward just like. Sittin' her down for an intervention."

"I think it would be an encounter session, in this instance."

"Whatever. Touchy-feely talking meeting." I give a big fake
shudder to make her laugh again but I'm not really lying, I
don't wanna have a feelings conversation with Bristol. I don't
wanna have a feelings talk with anybody. But I don't expect her
to be a robot either, we just should've realized that this was
too big, too soon. She's the one who got antsy. She also hasn't
done anything wrong; none of this is her fault. "Lord knows
she won't want to have that with us."

"True."

"Have you made any progress?"

"Well I think the reason this dog is so valuable is that she's from
the old lines or types that were somehow saved when China ordered all these dogs killed a long long time ago, which means
she's still a valuable outcross for the newer lines. And I think
somebody stole her."

I laugh, loud enough that I'm surprised I don't hear Bristol
reacting disapprovingly next door. It's not that kind of hotel,
though. "Yeah, Bits, *we* stole her."

"No, no, I mean. Stole her in the first place to auction her."

"Oh! Huh." Does it make more sense now, that Bristol's guy got shot? Was Bristol's guy working for the original owners? "That doesn't exactly clear anything up."

"It doesn't."

"Did you tell Bristol?"

"Yeah, I texted her. She says she's going to do her morning routine and then she'll open the between door."

"Makes sense." A morning routine. She doesn't mean like, pushups or walkouts or anything like I do. We've spent enough time traveling together to know each other's routines. Bits blinks at me, and her eyes look like her eyes but I know she did the cornea implants things so that she doesn't have to mess with contacts anymore, and I can't help but always look for them to catch the light weird or something. I knew people who got 'em early, that looked like that, but tech sometimes progresses in months, not even years anymore. Even with stuff like this. Especially if you're willing to go to a country with different regulations than maybe the U.S. has. No comment on where my arm came from.

I drink one of the beers from the mini bar then remember it's morning and make a pot of coffee. The dog starts wandering around, sniffing corners and whining. "I need to get her outside, this ain't a good way to keep her."

"She's *so* recognizable, Dolly, I don't—"

"Yeah I know but you can't make a dog live like this. When it was like twelve hours, that was one thing. Just gonna go out to the grass in the parking lot and back again, it'll be fine. What're the chances anybody looking for her thinks she's still here? And what're the chances they'd cruise past here what, for some gamblin' or luxury shopping?"

Bits sighs. "Okay."

I pick up the leash and the dog comes over eagerly. "Will you keep an eye out?"

"Of course. I'm not a panopticon though, I can't catch everybody who sees you."

"Yeah I know."

"Okay."

"Okay." We blink at each other, then I leash up the dog, poke my head out into the hallway to look both ways, and we skulk to the back staircase. So far so good.

I light a cigarette and wander around a little with the dog. Not very far, and on high alert, but it turns out okay. Bits doesn't say anything, nobody seems to particularly notice, and when she finishes up, we go back inside again, same way. I don't want to say it's a letdown, it's not like I'm jonesing for action. It's maybe also a little weird that this dog is so good with me, but I guess those hot dogs really did make us friends, who's to say.

I also feel like I need to start callin' her something. A real dog is a real dog and needs a name, unlike the robot dog, and I consider as we get down the hall and back to the suites. Ours is empty, and I go through the between doors to Bristol's. She cleaned up, and I feel kinda bad that she did it on her own, but I guess maybe Bits helped her last night. I didn't ask. There's also a room service trolly, with a pitcher of orange juice, no, I'll bet it's a pitcher of mimosas. "How we doing?"

"Better today, thank you" Bristol says.

"Look, Bristol, I'm sorry," I say, and she sips her mimosa and raises her eyebrows. "Bits and I have replacement shoes waitin' for you."

"You do know how to be very sweet, Dolly," she says, and there's the proper Bristol shell again. "I've been able to move on from that *mishap*," she quirks her lips a little and glances at the dog "to consider what steps we ought to take next."

"Oh that's good." I take a drink of mimosa; it's funny how something like beer isn't an okay breakfast beverage, but mimosas are. I've seen people go off their asses on mimosas without really trying. Only since meetin' Bristol, of course, champagne was thin on the ground back home, other than what people scavenged from wine caves sometimes. "What're you thinking?"

"Well probably simplest is we could unsteal the dog. Sneak it back into the facility and then it's just out of our hands." Bits and I exchange a look, and Bristol sighs. "I didn't say I prefer that option, only that it *is* one."

"Bitsy did you tell her what you thought?" Bits nods.

"She did, and that brings me to the next option. We go through my contact's electronics, locate his employer, and deliver the dog to them. They're the actual ones who hired us, after all. Surely they'll still wish to honor the deal."

"Surely." I look at Bits again, who shrugs.

"Well, I've already been working on that. First off, he didn't have any money on him, which is kind of interesting."

"Not even a crypto wallet?"

"Nope." Bristol seems visibly surprised. Bits gets a real paper map out of one of her pockets, and unfolds it. Oh, it's an AR enabled map, that's better; it means she can zoom it around and put down markers and stuff. "Okay, so from his phone we know where he was in Macau for the last few days. Before then he was in Da Nang, which is where he bought the phone, or at least where he started using it."

I finish my mimosa. They're always in smallish glasses, maybe that's why it's so easy to get blasted on them. I investigate the covered things on the breakfast cart and grab a plate of steak and eggs. The dog is now *very* interested in me. "So what, we get on a plane to Vietnam?"

"We haven't the papers to fly with the dog," Bristol says.

"We don't have the papers to travel with the dog at all," Bits points out. "That bag Dolly grabbed has the vaccine records, which might be good enough. But if we get stopped on the road someplace in China, we're gonna have a problem, because of the auction."

"Look, I like road trips, but a road trip from Macau to Vietnam seems a little much."

"It'd be shorter than Macau to Tibet," Bits says, reasonably.

"Well yeah but—"

"I *do* have the growing sense that we ought to leave Macau very soon," Bristol says, with that deliberate idleness that means it's a pressin' thought that she maybe shoulda mentioned immediately, but also we do tend to blow town once we get shot at. "We could just...borrow a boat and go across to Hong Kong."

"I don't disagree. Actually, since Hong Kong's self-governing, we'll at least have some breathing room to plan." Hong Kong is the emergency exit strategy I had in mind, actually. Barring Disney sovereignty. Besides, any one of us might know somebody in Hong Kong that can help us out. And even if we don't *personally* know anybody, we can always friend of a friend it.

"You do know how to drive a boat, don't you?" Bristol asks.

"Well yeah, I can pilot a boat." We try anything else, we run into the same papers problem, even on the official ferry I'm sure.

"Oh or a helicopter!" She's got that sparkle in her eyes now, oh boy.

"I like the boat option better," I say, as calm and dry as I can. "Haven't been shot out of the sky yet, and I'd like to keep that record shiny." Granted a helicopter to Hong Kong is an even shorter trip than by boat but. Like I said.

"Seconded," Bits says.

"Okay, so we're all in agreement, we're going to pack and get a boat?" Bristol asks.

"Yeah, we'll pack and get a boat," I say. Bits nods. "And we'll see who we know in Hong Kong to get us elsewhere."

"I'm sure that will be the simplest thing," Bristol says airily, and as a thought exercise, I really would love to have everybody's mental image of 'a boat' laid out in little AR popups to see what we each expect we're dealing with. Just to compare notes, you understand. Just like everybody's mental image of 'car' is gonna be different, or 'dog,' or 'apple.'

"Bitsy, what'd you find out about the guy's boss?"

"Well I didn't really find a boss, per se. I'm still combing through the data. Well, I wrote a program to comb through the data. I'm figuring out who to contact, and where they are."

"But we're certain they'll want the dog, so we might as well get to the right country," Bristol says, smiling.

"We don't really know that Vietnam's the right country," I say.

"However, we *do* know that we've finished our time in Macau."

"We sure do." I look at Bits, who's looking out the window. I look too, thinking wouldn't it just be fucking dandy if a helicopter hovered into view just outside, ready to open fire, but that doesn't happen. This time. Maybe I'll just call the dog Honey, the way she's all gold. We need to figure out how to travel with her, though. She's pretty recognizable. And then I think of all the appliances and shit that both the bathrooms have. Hair dryers. Curling irons. Clippers. I mosey over to my room to look, despite the private joy of imagining the look on Bristol's face if I shaved a dog in her hotel room.

Chapter Thirteen

O f course, it's one thing to decide to shave a dog, and another thing to shave a dog. She doesn't want to bite me, or us, and that's a lucky thing because I'm not really into being shredded open by an angry dog. Or being shredded open in general. It's kinda sometimes one of those occupational hazard things, the kind of thing you consider maybe reconsidering when you're in the bathtub in a swanky hotel suite with a dog who's as big as a person and who doesn't want any part of what you're doing. Yeah I made this choice.

Also, the clippers are the smart kind that don't cut skin, so that's another upside. And they have a dog setting. It's probably fuckin' sacrilege, to shave a dog like this down even a little, but it'd make her less recognizable. It's probably not great for a dog like this, to have her hair shaved very much.

I think I had the idea that being in the bathtub would keep the mess minimized but instead it made the clippers louder and was slick so made Honey nervous and so we get out of the tub pretty quick. Once I just let her stand on the bathmat, she minds the clippers less, and really, who knew that being a dog groomer was such a specialized thing? I guess they use tables, they have the dogs stand on tables. But she doesn't look too mangled when I'm done. We're all used to quarantine haircuts by now. She also doesn't really look like the same dog, which was the whole point. She's also got a tattoo in one ear, which

I never would've found otherwise, and I take a picture of that for Bitsy's files. And while we're still corralled in the bathroom, she comes in with the microchip scanner she kitbashed together from all her collected scraps, and we scan the regular place and then some irregular places lookin' for a chip, but don't turn one up. Which is interesting, because the auction catalog listed a chipped dog. Chips fail sometimes, sure, but I think all our guts're telling us this is something else.

"Dolly, I never would have expected you to be crafty like that!" Bristol exclaims while I'm doing the paracord, while Honey chews some apology jerky and Bits is, I assume, crunching on that dog tattoo data we got.

"It ain't exactly knitting," I say, because doing stuff with paracord is pretty utilitarian but also, we don't know everything about each other. Sometimes it's more obvious than others. Sometimes it matters more than others.

"No, but you could probably, I don't know, do hair."

"I don't think you want me doin' your hair like this, Bristles."

"Well no, but..." she trails off, but she's smiling like she's learned a secret. And it's nice to see her have that kind of sly smile again, honestly. Bristol's attractive in any number of ways, but it's not for nothing that I never mix business and that type of pleasure. Besides not being her type. I've seen her devastate men across the globe.

"Anyway, we all packed? Anything else we need?"

"I think we're good," Bits says.

"You got us a boat picked out, Bitsy? Any last minute data finds that'll make us change our mind?"

"I have a few boats in mind." She pauses, I guess to scan through some stuff. "And no. It seems like we're maybe on the right track."

"Well okay let's hit it."

I'm actually impressed with how little luggage Bristol has, but I guess with her veteran traveler status plus the kinda money we got floating around, she doesn't actually need to carry much. And a lot of her dresses like, vacuum pack down into eggs or something. I dunno. I always just roll a few pairs of jeans and tank tops and stuff into a duffle and call it good. Riot gear's most useful when it's on you, anyway, no sense having to worry about packing it.

This isn't to say Bristol doesn't have more luggage than the rest of us, but we don't need to hitch a cart to the dog to get it to the marina. And she carries it herself. I wonder, sometimes, how she got and stays so fit, without ever letting somebody see her break a sweat. She doesn't run. She doesn't go to a martial arts dojo or anything. Could she have just watched enough krav maga videos or something and learned it that way? There's other ways to hands-off learn something like that, my time in the not-quite-legit area of the military taught me that, but is any of it something Bristol would do? I actually think it's real important to not let yourself get too comfortable in what you assume people are willing to do. Limiting your estimations can be hazardous to your health.

And yeah, I kinda think Bristol would do a lot of things. Whether I've seen her do them or not. She got this way on her own sheer determination. And now that I've finally realized what that brittle edge she's had is all about, I'm just trying to keep an eye out, without being too obvious about it. Which probably means she knew about thirty seconds into this morning.

The dog's happily perched near the front of the boat like a figurehead, barking at the chop and wagging her tail, and I look at Bits, and she's already got her VR goggles on, making sure we aren't being APBed and targeted by militaries and flagged for bounty the second we're in international waters or something. Not like we can do a whole hell of a lot, depending on who comes after us. I feel pretty bad about not being able to put that handgun back where I got it, but I'll treat it good so long as I have it, and hopefully it won't be at the bottom of the ocean before all this is through.

"Bristol, you gonna be okay?" I finally ask. Then fumble for a reason I'm asking. "You normally get seasick?"

"I'm sure I'll be fine," she says, smoothing her skirt. Because of course she's dressed as though she's yachting and not as though we almost got shot last night. Over a dog. I nod and I wait. "No, I don't normally get seasick, and you know it."

"Check the cooler, see if there's ginger ale."

"Dolly, you don't need to baby me."

"I just know that you really enjoy feelin' like you're in the lap of luxury," I drawl. "And we ain't got the room for staff so..." She laughs, finally.

"Yes, I hadn't gotten around to hiring a personal assistant yet. They always require such *hand holding* and I just can't abide it." We've got the smile again, and I think I've distracted her enough. Which makes me wonder, is she acting like this on purpose to distract *me* from something, but if that's the case, that isn't a game I'm gonna win so I might as well just quit or play along. And we're in the middle of the...what body of water is this. The South China Sea, and there ain't a lot of quitting options. Not unless some pirates swing by and I join up or something. We probably should've thought about the whole possibility of pirates. I don't think they tend to have rocket launchers out here, though, that's more of an Indian Ocean thing.

The dog gets bored with the waves eventually and makes her way over to Bits, who pretty much hasn't moved since we've come aboard, and curls up at her feet. I play some music in my earbuds, then I wonder if we can get any kind of radio signal out here and scan for that too. Mostly static, a couple blips from maybe submarines or other boats or something. It's hard to know, what it'll grab sometimes. Not like I listen to numbers stations as a hobby, the way some people do, but the fact that it's viable is truly a thing of beauty.

Actually, now that I'm thinking about it, submarines could be a thing we should worry about. Not 'cause of the dog people, but because of who we crossed during the business with the diamonds. Shit, wouldn't that be something, thinking we're home free to cash in on this reverse dognapping and then a sub surfaces with that Will guy coming out of the hatch.

We used to do that a lot, me and my...well if we were real sanctioned military we'd be called a unit. Me and the guys. The ones who were part of the black site, "what if we put these various cybernetics in people with a certain type of training?" and the "what if we gave people this kind of training?" and "what about these injections?" and "what about this muscle density without increasing any apparent mass?" Those guys. We'd be bored somewhere, doing exercises, because all we ever really ended up doing was training exercises, canned deployment exercises, for the people with clipboards and the brass whose faces we never saw. We'd be bored, and we'd come up with worst case scenarios in as much exquisite detail as we could muster, and we'd then turn to somebody and say like "Hey Cash, wouldn't it be something if..." or "Hey Trigger, do you think somebody ever..." and lay whatever it was out. And everybody'd be like "nah" or they'd join in. Good times.

So we're all within earshot of each other but I gotta pick one and Bitsy looks busy even if maybe she isn't so I say "Hey Bristol, wouldn't it be something if..." and she suddenly looks up and off to the side, and then shades her eyes even though she's wearing sunglasses, and she says

"Ladies, do we think that's going to be a problem?" in a deliberately casual tone and I wonder if I've conjured a submarine into existence by my habit of whistling past the graveyard. If that's what whistling past the graveyard even means. Does anybody know what that means? And anyway, it's hard to be anywhere that's never been a graveyard. There's probably sunken ships under us right now, even if there isn't a sub. What Bristol's pointing at isn't a sub.

I can't help it, and laugh. "We got problems with that, it's 'cause whoever's at the helm ends up blind," I say. Bristol looks a little hurt, and I realize my eyes're better than hers. I forget about that, despite everything else. The eye thing is more subtle; not all AR and stuff like Bits's, just...better. "Sorry, sorry. It's a cargo ship."

"You could have said so," she says, a little primly.

"Hey I said I'm sorry."

"You two will argue about anything," Bits says, blinking at us.

"Yeah, prob'ly." Actually, a cargo container ship would be a great way to do a whole lotta things. How many helicopters could take off and land on a cargo container ship, even if it appeared totally packed to the gills from our remove. "So, not right now, but do you think—"

"Please no," Bits says.

"You didn't even listen to what I was gonna say!"

She looks from me, to the ship, and back again. "Do I need to?"

"I guess not." I grin, and Bristol laughs softly.

Chapter Fourteen

⸻

We spend the day at sea, snacking on Bristol's canned caviar and some kind of cheese spread and a whole lot of crackers and yeah, some beers. The crossing from Macau doesn't really take that long, but when you're tryin' to be *clandestine*, sometimes it means screwing around for awhile to run out the clock. We find a quiet place to dock when it's just around sunset. I've actually never been up and about Hong Kong in the daytime; what an experience that'd be. Maybe someday. Bits does something that sends the boat away again, I guess maybe it can get itself back to Macau, or close enough, and make it so we really didn't put the owner out much. I dunno. Some people own a whole bunch of boats and never even use them much. They probably wouldn't've even noticed, until time came to pay rent on the slip and it was empty, and then they would've filed insurance, and that would've been that. Practically a victimless crime.

"Bitsy, see about an Airbnb or whatever for tonight. No hotel, I don't think." I rub my shoulder next to my neck; scab's itchy and I shouldn't scratch it.

"Only tonight?" Bristol asks. She's real careful, there's only a little bit of disappointment, or disapproval, in her voice. The shopping, the night life, the fish pedicures. Probably something else, but we gotta keep this moving. At least she had time to pick up the replacement shoes before we went to sea.

"We're still too close, and anyway, it's pretty possible that who-ever took shots at us came here too. I'm just looking for our out."

"I'll look for a place near Disney," Bits says. "Less chance of snipers."

"Good call, House of Mouse has its own mercenaries."

"They do *not*." Now Bristol's a mix of scandalized and delight-ed.

"They do. I interviewed once but ultimately figured it wasn't for me."

"You did not," she says. I grin at her.

"I absolutely, one hundred percent did. But now you'll always have that doubt and it'll drive you nuts." It's true, I did. The Florida park did a combination of like, sea walls and moats that protected it when the water came up. And they've got a bunch of underwater rides now. They didn't call me back after the in-terview.

"You are extremely wicked and I have no idea why we are asso-ciates," she huffs, but she's still smiling.

"We show off each other's best qualities." Honey has been standing with me patiently through all this, looking up at us as we talk and panting a little. It is hot here, hotter than it was on the open ocean. Sea. Open water. Did shaving her down a little help with that? Or was the fur protective? How hot does it get in Tibet, anyway? I could look it up but really, I pretty much prefer to wonder, and talk it out with somebody. I know Bits goes and learns the answer to a question the second it comes across her synapses but it's nice to wonder sometimes, about some things. It's nice to not know. I wonder which Bristol does. Probably a little bit of both. See, with Bristol and me, even if we *do* look something up, it's in a totally normal search engine way. Bits can do that I'm sure, but she can also do the 'oh I found a closed door, let's see what's inside' way. And does.

"Okay, found one," Bits says.

"Good, I'll walk you over there and then see about our airlift."

Bristol arches an eyebrow like she's practiced it in the mirror. I'm sure she has. "Walk us over?"

"You wanna walk the dog? If you do, I can just..." She looks down at Honey and sighs.

"Not with *that* haircut, I don't. The poor thing."

"Aw, sorry, her usual hairdresser was otherwise occupied. I guess. Probably." I grin, and Bristol rolls her eyes elaborately. Bits hides a smile. "C'mon. I want to be able to take advantage of the night life."

Lodgings, check. They pick where to order delivery, check. And I've already got the weapons I found in Macau; the gun seems fine after our swim, and I had fresh ammo for it just in case. Pretty much as prepared as I'm gonna get, without a rolodex for criminal and criminal-adjacent pilots that I know who happened to be in Hong Kong just now who also have their own aircraft. I actually got a couple people in mind, and a couple places to look for them. I get a taxi over to one of the night markets, My Cantonese is *okay*, better than most of the guys' French ever ended up being. Better than my Japanese.

The market's crowded, but the market is always crowded. I look at the food stands and little bars and things as I pass them, try to gauge the types of people eating there. Most of them normal types, not like me. Not the kind of person I need. I'm really not expecting to see a familiar face here, so when I do, I just keep walking for a few steps, like in a comedy bit, and then I stop, ruining the flow of foot traffic. Dunno if it would've been wilder to see one of my sisters or brothers, who I haven't talked to in awhile, or if it's wild enough that it's Butler, who I was just thinking about last night.

I turn around, though, and he's coming out of the little restaurant just looking shocked, and I can't help but laugh. The other marketgoers just part around us rude people standing in the walkway lookin' at each other and I get my laugh and he gets over his shock and closes the distance between us with a couple of long strides, takes me by the shoulders and looks me in the face. "Dolly it's been forever."

"I guess it has," I say. "Feels like it, anyway." Couple years, maybe.

"You could've called."

I pull back, punch him in the shoulder. "Oh don't pull that sad puppydog shit, *you* could've called."

He actually rubs the contact spot a little, and I try to remember what upgrades I had the last time we saw each other. Definitely not the new arm. Definitely most of the muscle and endocrine stuff. "Geeze, don't know your own strength." He's kind of grinning, kinda shaking his head, and I grin right back.

"Trust me, I know." I wonder if he's imagined a reunion. I wonder if he thought we'd run to each other like all those movies with people running to each other across a meadow. I'm imagining the love story Bristol thinks would be going on here, and really, all of those things aren't really very near to the truth. Maybe in another life, if we were different people.

"I'll always trust you," he said, voice a little too serious. I blink at him. Right this second isn't the right time to look and see if he's wearing that belt buckle. "But enough small talk, what's going on? What're you doing here?"

"I could ask you the same thing."

"So ask, it'd be nice to see you taking an interest. Come on, I'll buy you a beer." I follow him back to his table at the little restaurant, let him order me a beer, partake of the plates of food he's got. Bristol's at-sea picnic was awhile ago, and it's gonna be awhile yet before I get to eat whatever takeout they picked out for me.

"You're kitted out," he says after my beer comes.

"Course I am, I'm working." Granted, I'm not wearing the jacket while we're sitting here, have it hung on the back of my chair. It's hot as hell even at night. "And what about you, just being a tourist?" He isn't kitted out, just jeans and a tee shirt, same old boots. You can always recognize my crowd by our boots, I feel like. Laces that the plastic tips never stay on, but we always pick the plastic tipped ones, never the metal. That thing has a name, doesn't it?

"Kind of touring, kind of scouting. What's the job?" He drops his eyes to my neck, where I left a bandanna tied, which has never been my habit. Yes, it's a clean one. Or was when I put it on this morning.

"Mmm, well it's a long story. Know any pilots in town?"

"I might." He gives me that old appraising look, sips on his beer. "You need more hands?"

"We've pretty much got it covered." What are the outcomes, if I bring Butler into this? Helps us with the dog wrangling, Butler's always been good with dogs, though I think I've handled her pretty well. It gives Bristol fresh material to work with; she'd be just wild to meet him, actually. Even more so if she thinks we're an item, or thinks we were ever an item. Nothing that's more than just companionship.

"Who's we?"

"Nobody you know." That's the downside, he's a little too interested. And he's solid, of course, or else I wouldn't be giving him the time of day right now. Our crew worked well, with our after-army ventures. After we couldn't just go home again, 'cause what was home anymore. If the world was different, we'd be married already, have a house somewhere, normal jobs, maybe kids. Maybe that's still possible and maybe I don't care about that. Maybe normal jobs never would've been something I'm suited for. I don't really think so. But I can never tell, and don't give me any of that biological clock bullshit about the kids. God knows we can hack and adjust and replace about everything else, of course it's on the list. "But anyway, we need a plane to Da Nang and can't just get on an airline and don't want to just road trip."

"Must be serious, if *you* don't want to road trip."

"Butler, for the love of god." It's just banter and I'm not mad, but there's a time crunch here, real or imagined.

"Sorry, sorry." He's smiling in a way that says he remembers the old days, and that's bullshit too, it was five years ago tops. Six. Seven. We aren't grizzled veterans; for all our scars, we're still pretty shiny and new. Lot of us were still practically kids, back when. Is there an appropriate time to tell somebody you had to get an arm replaced? If there's etiquette for that, Bristol'd know. "I know a couple people, sure. I've been working some guys are running a bootleg helicopter joint, and doing some side projects along the way."

Bootleg helicopters, that's sure a thing people try sometimes. Plus I'm startin' to think that my brain was messed with more than I thought, there keep being more coincidences than I'm happy with. I been thinking about helicopters since we got here and now...this. They did test us for, what'd they call it, precognitive abilities. Put us in VR of being in a room looking at a door when the doorbell rings, and it was fifty fifty whether there was a man with a gun on the other side of the door. Most of us did worse than fifty-fifty, me included, except the one time, right before they cut that part of the program off, where the doorbell rang and I was convinced right down to my bones that there was a man with a gun on the other side of that door, 100%, it was real and he had a gun, and I was right. Well except it wasn't real it was VR. Oh I should tell Bits about that, I don't think I ever did. "That's real interesting and all but I don't think we can take a helicopter from here to Vietnam?"

"You might. Vietnam's closer than you think." I sigh and finish my beer. "Anyway, they're gonna know other pilots, even if you don't showcase one of their models."

"Okay, good. That's good. We'll pay them, of course."

"Of course." He gestures at the person behind the counter for more beers. "And what about me?" Aglets, that's what the things on laces're called. Aglets go through eyelets.

I raise my eyebrows at him. "What about you?"

Chapter Fifteen

I message Bits while me and Butler are walking to the helicopter place, or maybe just where the helicopter people live.
Sure I've known him for a lifetime but, people change, so I
wanna give her the space to check and see if Butler's actually
got nefarious connections and aims, but everything seems on
the level, or at least still our type of crooked. //Who is this
guy?// she asks.

//Somebody I know from home.// I glance at him; he must assume I've gotta make contact with my people, but he's not even
lookin at me, but out the cab window. //Look he knows some
helicopter people, and even if one of their rides doesn't work,
they know other pilots.//

//Sounds good.// And I think that's that but then Bits messages me again. //So Bristol is really excited that you're bringing a man home so I guess be prepared for that.//

//Great. Roger that.// I assumed she'd be like this, it's fine.
I'd be more worried if she wasn't, honestly. //I'll let you know
when we're done and heading over.//

"You just got in today, you said?" Butler asks.

"Yeah, I haven't even seen the inside of the place yet. I came
right to the market after dropping 'em off."

"Over by Disney you said? Was prob'ly pretty pricey."

"Right?" I grin at him; he's fishing and it's none of his goddamn business. Bringing a man home. I never brought Butler home, at home. He *was* home, if that makes any kinda sense. All the families knew each other, at home, all the families worked together, at home, because survival was work besides the other stuff that we did to get money for what we couldn't just do for ourselves. All us kids just ran in a feral barefoot herd as we grew up, playing and scrapping and all of that, boys and girls alike. Sometimes people peeled off for more domestic pursuits and sometimes we got caught up in cybernetic super soldier programs, it's just how it is. How it was. Well. We signed up for it. We thought it'd be good for our families.

I assume he messages his guys too, and where the cab leaves us is definitely not a place where helicopters are stored or manufactured, it's still right in the city, an apartment building with stories and stories of rocking and crackling and humming AC units perched on the outside like the weirdest squarest pigeon problem. Seems like all the renewable energy people would be really into figuring out a better way for environmental controls planetside; they got it figured out in space after all.

The elevator's got an Out Of Order sign written on it on cardboard and we go up the stairs, and then up the stairs, and then up the stairs. The building's pretty quiet, probably everybody else sleeping. I don't really know where the time went but it's to that time of night where most decent people're sleeping and people like us have drunk too much, or done other things too much, and are going about our business in a way that we tend not to in daylight, even though we could I guess. Bothers me less than a lotta people. Bits isn't super into light in general, she's practically mole people sometimes. Not normally so bad as when we drove back up through Mexico, finished off that job with Bristol and Nicolai.

Butler's got a real actual key for the door and lets himself in. The door opens to a little hallway where shoes are lined up, and he kicks out of his unlaced boots, and I kick out of mine. I get a closer look, of course; they are definitely the same kind of laces. Old habits. Same socks too.

"Hello!" a gangly Asian guy in a coverall with the sleeves rolled up comes in the hallway and waves. I become aware of a repeating, high-pitched noise just at the edge of my hearing, maybe a fan, maybe some weird AC unit, but no, the AC units here are humming. "I'm Meatball."

"Dolly," I say, waving back.

"Scooter went out to get beers," Meatball says to Butler.

"Aw, they didn't have to do that."

Meatball scratches the back of his neck, shrugs. "Sure they did. *We* did." He's got mechanic's hands, scuffed and scarred, and his eyes have the replacement-glints that Bitsy's do now. I wonder if his are recent, or if they're post-market the way mine would've been, if I had 'em.

"Well I appreciate it," I say. In the apartment now, there's a couple closed doors but mainly this living room I think, and a row of 3D printers on a long low table against one wall, their arms all moving. That's the noise. None of 'em are really big enough to be printing big helicopter parts, but I'm sure there's lotsa small stuff that they can piece out here. Or other things that they can make faster and sell faster to support the helicopter habit. Everything's orderly, though. Tidier than I'd known Butler to be, so either he doesn't live here, or he pitches in. Or they let him take care of other things. Lots of possibilities. Lots of people willin' to do housework for you, if you take care of occasional necessary violence for them. As me how I know.

"See? Somebody knows about hospitality!" Meatball says, and Butler actually chuckles.

"Yeah, Dolly hung some manners on somewhere," he said. Did I? Kinda. Bristol's manners by osmosis, maybe. "When we were kids, though..."

"I don't think we need to revisit that era," I say. God we're gonna go over this again in the rental with Bits and Bristol, aren't we. Maybe we'll be late enough that Bristol will be asleep, anyway. Then we can at least all face it fresh with the morning.

"You knew each other when you were kids? That's so cool!"

"Sure did! And Butler's the biggest mama's boy you ever did know. Every little bump or scrape, he'd go runnin' home from wherever we were, sometimes across the whole damn county, so she'd kiss it and make it better." I smile sweetly when Meatball laughs, and wander over to the printers as Butler defends his manliness.

"She's always been this mean, as you can guess."

"Sure have." They've got all kinds of little parts going on the printers. Valves and clamps and other fiddly things. One of them is definitely gun parts, not really a surprise. Gotta print what pays, I assume. Or maybe it's a one-off, maybe they started it when Butler called 'em because they didn't have any guns on hand. I guess that's possible. Scooter and Meatball could be wide-eyed innocents in this terrible world, just helicopter enthusiasts. With their good new friend Butler. Hmm.

There's a key in the lock and I glance at Meatball and Butler; Butler was looking at me already and our eyes meet for a moment. I don't know what his play is here, I shouldn't assume he's got one, and I shouldn't mess up whatever it is. We just need a ride, preferably sooner rather than later, preferably as discreet as a bootleg helicopter can be.

Scooter comes in cautiously, a little less vigorous than Meatball, but they do smile and hold up the beers. "I bought two six packs of Hong Kong Machine Men."

"Sounds exciting, thanks a ton," I say. Really, what I know about Hong Kong beers is that there's a bunch of breweries here, actually, and that Party is the one that people really don't like. There's probably more but no matter how fun it sounds, Party beer is not where it's at. Kinda like mandatory fun. Nobody wants that.

"You're welcome! Any...friend of Butler's is a friend of ours!" Scooter pulls out one of the bottles and hands it to me. Well that was a weird pause.

"Aw well thanks." I look at Butler, and look at Butler's belt buckle then. Yup, it's the old spur one. He sees me looking and grins. I lever my bottle cap off with the offered opener; probably a table edge would've been fine, but you don't do that when you're a guest in somebody's house unless they do it first. Plus, no sense showing off my cyber strength unless I have to, doin it with my bare hands. "So did he tell you why I'm in town?"

"Only that you need a ride to Vietnam and he offered one of our helicopters?" Scooter says, looking slightly worried. "Which, not that we *mind* really, except that—"

"I didn't offer to give her a helicopter, I said that we could maybe arrange a ride," Butler says with a laugh.

"And we'll pay," I say. "We're not lookin' to take advantage of anybody. Well. We're not lookin' to take advantage of *you.*"

Scooter looks less worried, and Meatball looks even more delighted. "From here to Vietnam? Where in Vietnam?"

"We were thinking Da Nang, but really, if you can get us in-country, we can figure it out from there." We're all of us pretty good, directionally. For different reasons, I guess.

"If we're taking your money to fly you to Vietnam we aren't going to just drop you off *wherever*," Scooter says, just total genuine disbelief.

"Hey, I'm not castin' aspersions on your professionalism. I just know plans have to change midstream sometimes, it's how things go."

"Okay but how much money are you going to pay us to fly you to Vietnam?" Meatball asks, maybe with visions of new 3D printers in his head, who can say. Of the two, I think Meatball's the dreamer. Probably also the impulsive one.

"Oh I dunno. I think just an airplane ticket is a couple hundred bucks nowadays. Let's say we'll cover your fuel and refuel, and then..." I watch Butler watching them and wonder what his play here is. He isn't here out of the goodness of his heart, that just isn't how he operates. Which isn't to say there isn't any good in him, he isn't the villain of many stories that I know about. God knows none of us're without sin; that's not even Tragic Backstory, just plain hard truth. Where we're from, it's too far from the coast to've flooded and too far from cities to've benefitted and just the infrastructure crumbled when they built the hyperloop and stuff, and when factory farms kept buying out the family ones and then going vertical. Time marched on. "How about ten thousand dollars."

That might still be too little, we might be takin' advantage, I do have more than that liquid. But Scooter makes a visible effort to decide to play it cool, and for a second, I wonder what a whole damn helicopter costs to buy, anyway, bootleg or not. I think, of the two, Scooter's the worrier. The planner. "Well I think that sounds about right, between the fuel, and then the maintenance we'll have to do once we get to Vietnam, and after we get home again. Plus our discretion of course."

"Plus your discretion," I agree, then I hold out my sweating beer bottle. "Drink to it?"

Scooter and Meatball look at each other, and Meatball has far less of a poker face and grins. Scooter shrugs, and we clink bottlenecks. "Drink to it."

Chapter Sixteen

====

Me and Butler walk to the Air B&B a couple hours later, after we get the plan hashed out. The beers weren't enough to get us drunk, but the bottle of rice liquor Scooter and Meatball *also* poured to us sure helped a lot, supersoldier livers or not. It's a good buzz, we're still more than combat ready should that become a necessity. I have a brief image of gettin' in some kind of weird brawl with police along the way, but that doesn't end up happening. We see police, sure, but they go their way and we go ours.

It's a nice walk. It's cooler at night, I guess, but still humid, so it still feels like you're moving around in a big mouth. The street lights all have these condensation puffballs around them like dandelions gone to seed. It's nice to be walking with Butler again; I missed him, but also it wouldn't've been all that hard for either of us to find the other and reconnect. We're not a tragic love story, just a tired one. Another life, another situation, we'd already have the house and picket fence and 2.5 kids or whatever. Dog and cat and electric minivan and lake cottage for summers. Little league games and lemonade stands and dance recitals. That stuff all still exists, right? Maybe not lemonade stands; too many kids were gettin' tickets for not having food service licenses or whatever bullshit. Like come *on*.

Instead, we got injections, and replacements, and playing soldier. Found out later some people got VR training. Some people got memory training. I dunno what the control group was; the history of modern warfare to that point, I guess. We got training and testing and more training and more tests and war games that we were all actually real good at. We also assumed that doing all that would help our families, protect our town, let them keep on keepin' on. The program kinda petered out and we were cut loose and that's when we found out it wasn't really the case. Nothing big bad happened, just the usual kind of everything slowly dried up and everybody blew away. Usual now, anyway; I guess it probably didn't used to be. Or maybe it's always been there, when you peel back the gold foil wrapping of The American Dream. Who can say.

Butler's not much of a talker, even when buzzed, and I think he expects me to grill him on what he's doing with Scooter and Meatball, if he's taking advantage of them or actually really into this helicopter thing, and when I don't, just kinda settle into my own thoughts as we walk, he doesn't really know what to do with himself. Eventually, after time looking at me out of the corners of his eyes, he clears his throat. I wait, and he does it again, and then he says "So you like the kids?"

"Yeah, they seem good, real smart. How'd you meet them?" They seem...I don't want to say young, that ain't it. And Meatball's got a shock of gray in his hair. They still seem hopeful, I guess. They aren't all scarred up and jaded. Or anyways, not visibly.

"They were at a weapons expo."

"3D printed guns?"

"Yeah. They're really into the theoreticals of that, but real squeamish about the idea that guns, y'know, shoot things. People."

"I can imagine." I can't remember when I still had a problem with that, necessarily. It just always seems like it was part of our reality. I just think it's a responsibility, that one should take care with. I got the scars that say I've been on the other end of people not takin' so much care with it. Or, they thought they were, without a doubt, in the right. I can sympathize with that. "And so they thought of the helicopters or..."

"Well you know how those things are, they sell all kinds of things."

"They do."

"And we got to talking..."

"And drinking."

"Yeah, and drinking." He looks at me and laughs. "And we bought a helicopter, and they already had a pretty good scanner for the rendering software so..."

"So you kinda accidentally fell into the bootleg helicopter business."

"Kinda."

"Got tired of shootin' people?" Like I'm one to talk, really. It's not like I don't still end up shooting people. Just my choice now, typically. The category of people, the type of rounds. Not that our little group of playing pretend super soldiers did a whole lotta shooting but. Well we didn't always know where they put us, or whether the rounds were live.

"Didn't say I gave that up. But you know how it is." He don't look haunted, exactly. I'm not sure any of us have that capacity, not after. But yeah. I know, and I nod, and he takes that as good enough. "So tell me about who you work with, don't let me walk in there with no intel."

"Damn, I thought I'd get away with it." We both laugh, and I think about it. What does he need to know. "Bristol's a flashy one, and smart as hell. Don't let her fool you with any kind of airhead act, and don't let her get you hooked either."

"You know who my heart belongs to." He's being dramatic, but is he?

I roll my eyes, I can't help it. "Shit, don't be like that."

"Noted."

"And Bits tends to be pretty quiet, and she's the smartest person I ever met. And I like and respect both of 'em and I'll eat your liver and your eyeballs if you upset them in any way." We used to say that all the time when we were kids; the big threat, too ridiculous to really understand, too scary to risk.

He puts his hands up, grinning a little lopsided. "I didn't realize it was that serious, I'll be on my best behavior."

"You'd better."

When we get there, I go in first and Honey barks once, big boom, and then comes to greet me. It's a really nice place, actually, and I wonder what we paid for it. I wonder if it's actually somebody's home for any of the time, or if it would normally be a local rental that somebody just uses for the online short term rentals like this. I rub behind the dog's ears, surprised and kinda pleased with myself that she's happy to see me. I should've at some point thought about how I should be careful to not get attached.

"Dolly, aren't you going to introduce us?" Bristol asks a little coyly, and I give her kind of a 'well maybe' grin and then shrug.

"This is Butler. Butler, this is Bristol and Bits."

"Lots of B names," Butler says carefully.

"Oh, the A names were all boring," Bristol says breezily, and Bits just kinda shrugs. "It's nice to finally meet you!"

"Finally?" he looks at me.

"I might've told stories, I honestly don't remember. You know how I get to running my mouth sometimes." Or she's fishing. Whichever, there's not a lot of harm in it. Probably.

"Might've told stories," he says slowly, laughing a little. "Well there's lots of those to go around. I'm sure you've even got some of your own."

"I'm very certain we do," Bristol says.

Bits knows what I'm about, though, and brings me to the kitchen where my food is. Also a range of beverages, I guess the fridge was stocked. Or one of them went out. I grab a bottle of water, and whatever my bag of food is, and call "Butler, you want anything? Coffee? Soda? Water? Beer?"

"Probably good to switch to coffee," he says after a brief pause. He'd better be careful, Bristol's getting him mesmerized. I warned him.

"Sure thing." I start to juggle stuff around to get a hand free and Bits laughs at me.

"I'll get it," she says, and gets a canned coffee out of the fridge. He'll take it just however, prefers it black or at least trained himself to drink it black. We all did, at one point. Couldn't rely on sweetener after the bees were gone, or creamer for about forever. The powdered stuff is surprisingly good, anyway. Well I think so. Prob'ly just thinking about it'd give Bristol hives or the vapors or something.

Back in the other room, Butler's in a chair and Honey pressed herself against his knees and is grinning up at him as he scruffs his big hands around in her fur, her eyes half closed.

"What, I invite you here, you steal my dog?" I toss him the coffee and he catches it, pops the tab.

"*Your* dog?"

"Nah, not really. I've just been on animal handlin' duty since we got her."

"And you are indeed the one who got her," Bristol says pointedly. Butler catches it but doesn't understand, looks between us, drinks his coffee.

"Sure did." I grin until Bristol cracks a smile and then returns her attention to Butler.

"So how long have you and Dolly known each other?"

"Oh, just about forever," Butler says. I start shoveling food, nod with my mouth full. He isn't gonna say anything that embarrasses me. There isn't anything that embarrasses me. Bits must've remembered that I liked ramen, or they both remembered that it doesn't matter what I eat, because they got me some kind of bright yellow, spicy noodles with little shrimps in it. Other meats too. My lips go numb pretty quick and it's really great actually. Spicy food is great after beer. And whatever that other stuff was. "How long have you ladies known each other?"

"A few years now, I'd say?" Bristol glances at both of us and Bits kind of nods. I'm sure Bits has a datestamp of our first encounter. Maybe even recordings squirreled away on some server or another, encrypted from here to the moon.

"But I guess you don't base outta Hong Kong."

"You know we don't. Quit fuckin' fishing," I say. Honey folds her ears at my tone, and I rub her flank with the side of my foot.

"Sorry, sorry. Old habits, y'know. Plus, what we do? You want to stay informed."

I laugh. "What you do is bootleg helicopters."

"Right now."

"Fair enough." I'm a little surprised Bristol is satisfied to just watch this interplay, but of course she is, it's like she's a predator drone that needs to take readings and calibrate.

"So is that really all you need, a helicopter ride?"

"Sure is," I say. "Told you to stop fishing."

"Well if he's offering *help*," Bristol says sweetly.

"Bristles I already paid for the damn helicopter, if you wanna pay for whatever Butler ends up costin' us you can go right ahead."

Butler leans back in his chair, folds his arms behind his head. "Who says I wanted you to hire me?"

"There's other ways ya end up having to pay sometimes." He pulls a hurt expression, boo hoo. I finish my noodles, take the garbage to the kitchen where I think I saw a can, Honey padding along behind me. Bits has to have worked her magic, found Bristol's contact's contact by now. I can hear Bristol's tone of voice, less her words, but that rise and fall of diverting and soothing. If he was a riled up horse, he'd be eating carrots out of her hand by the time I got back. It's just the banter, always has been, but anytime we add somebody to the mix, the dynamic has to shake out and settle down.

"Okay, so the plan is we get our flight plan in, load everybody up, and take you away from all this," Butler says when I come back.

"Oh well good. Gotta love a cakewalk."

"You know better than to say that," Bits mutters.

"Sure do!" I smile big and Butler laughs. Bristol smiles, but in that brittle-edged way that means she doesn't particularly like where this is going, and I can definitely see how it'd seem from her perspective. "Anyway, when will we be in the air you think? I'd say wheels up, but..."

"It typically takes a day to get flight plans approved," Butler says.

"So day after tomorrow? Elizabits, you think you could..."

"On it," she says.

"Just like that?" Butler asks.

"Sometimes," she says, getting up and going to what I assume is a bedroom.

"Bristol, do we know anything more about the Vietnam end of things?"

"I put in a call to a contact," she says, maybe a little carefully. She doesn't know what I told Butler, and doesn't want to have to explain the whole thing I'm sure. I didn't want to have to explain the whole thing, so I didn't. "They're going to get back to me in the morning."

"Perfect." I stretch, and yawn. "Well I gotta go to sleep. I guess I'll empty the dog first, yeah."

I can't even describe the looks that cross Bristol's face in rapid succession, but she makes some noise of agreement and retires. I find the leash, get Honey hooked up, and she and Butler follow me outside. "So you're just reuniting this dog with the owner or what?" he asks, quietly.

"That's the plan!" I say. "We thought it'd happen in Macau but...lost our contact."

"Lost your contact," he says, like he's thinking about it. It doesn't take him long, though, I see it in his face when we pass under a streetlight. I see somethin' else there that makes me wonder a little. Side jobs. "Well that's rough."

"Only Bristol knew him, and only a little. Friend of a friend. But yeah it was a surprise, definitely." Dangerous as this line of work is, we don't lose people often, somehow. I guess if we did, we would've stopped before now, providin' we were smart enough. I'd like to think we're smart enough. Back doin' army stuff, we lost people a couple times. Officially, on the books, we were only ever experimental, and only ever playin' war games. In reality, they put us in the shit a couple of times. Very expensive, very expendable; a real weird combination, I always thought. Though I also always thought it was real weird that they just cut us loose, instead of pushin' some red button that made something self destruct. Though I guess with the post-hypnotic stuff, we're considered mothballed. I should've thought of that sooner, that I'm deprogrammed but Butler ain't.

Honey does her business, and we walk back to the air b&b. He hangs out at the bottom of the steps like he's come callin' and is too bashful or too mindful of my dad with a shotgun to come up and kiss me, and I gotta smile at that. "You gonna ask me to stay the night?" he asks.

"You know, I don't think I am. But I'll see you tomorrow." I pull the bandanna off my neck to see the look on his face, then wave it and blow him a kiss. Yeah, he looks, has a little twitch of the lips, then he recovers and laughs, shaking his head.

"Goodnight, Dolly."

"'Night Butler."

Chapter Seventeen

B utler texts me in the morning, right around dawn actually, that we got our flight clearance for 1100. Sure we're programmed to be early risers, but he could've waited a little while. I go to roll over, but Honey's sprawled across my legs, and she doesn't move but she does groan. I lay back for a sec, and laugh, because what else are you gonna do if a Tibetan Mastiff is layin' on you and doesn't want to wake up? I can move her. I'm gonna move her. But there's no harm in lettin' her get a few more minutes of shuteye. We should probably look into some kind of doggie tranquilizer for the chopper ride, I'm pretty damn sure she isn't gonna just go along with it otherwise. I message that to Bits, she'll find me a pharmacy or something.

Eventually I just doze off again, and eventually Butler messages me again and it's a picture of a dog kennel strapped in the back of a helicopter, Scooter and Meatball giving thumbs ups from the open doors. This time I groan, and then I send back a thumbs up, and then I get to work gettin' Honey to move. She's more amiable this time, has to go out, and I smoke a cigarette while we're at it, for the up and at 'em and for the memory of...who was that? Butler's dad and one of his brothers, rigging up a trailer to bring home a steer they'd won at auction because they were the only bidders. Of course that particular steer had never been loaded on a trailer a day in his life, much less one held together with wire and future thoughts of barbecue.

131

When I get back inside, Bits is blearily poking at the coffee machine, and Bristol is breezing about the place in a cloud of flowery perfume. She's actually in riot gear, which is good, I didn't wanna have to fight with her about wearing high heels in a helicopter. Of course her boots are black velvet, but I know they're leather too, and a good brand. So long as it's fashion *and* function, I don't give a fuck. She isn't stupid; she's very interested in self preservation, so we're all on the same page there.

"We all packed?" I ask. "Tasers charged, dragonscale on?" Other than getting shot at, this whole thing has been a little too calm, actually. Other than bickerin' with each other. I won't say I got jitters, exactly, but the anticipation adrenaline has a little more edge to it. Hopefully it'll stay boring, we'll just have a big long chopper ride and then that'll be that. Whistle through your teeth and spit, I guess.

"Yeah, we're ready. Do you want to order breakfast or what?" Bits asks.

"If you're wondering if I'm hungry, fuck yes. If you think that I think we should wander out for street food with a stolen dog, no. So yeah, let's order in. Bristol can pick the place."

"How very generous of you," Bristol says cheerfully. She already knows what she wants, it's fine. We all know I don't care what I eat.

"Hey, I got my moments." I didn't really unpack in the first place, but I repack what I did. Make sure all the dog's stuff is packed. Give the house a general once-over, make sure we're not leaving anything vital. It's not like it's really feasible to do a forensic sweep or anything, remove all our fingerprints and loose hairs and stuff, but not leaving a big sign with flashing fluorescent lights sayin' who we are and why we're here is also good. If somebody on our trail looked around this apartment, would they find anything out, other'n what we ordered for food? What soap Bristol prefers? Doesn't seem like it. Leave only footprints, they say but...lotta times, you don't want to even do that.

//So where's the meetup?// I text Butler. Chances're about zero that Scooter and Meatball just have a helipad on their apartment building's roof, unless their bootleg helicopters are also stealth. He doesn't answer in words, just a set of coordinates, and I forward them to Bits.

//See you soon// he says after a few minutes and I just send him a plus sign because Bristol is making that 'can't we just have a nice meal for once?' face and no of course we can't, but sometimes we pretend for her. It's not the same as lying, exactly.

Breakfast is good, of course it is, and then Bits sends me a file that's part of the care 'n' feeding of this dog and for flying, that involves sedation sorts of pills that's in her kit that I also stole, and I haven't put pills in many things other than people, but I hide it in a piece of hot dog and it goes down fine. It's a double-edged sword, givin' a dog that big knockout pills. You need to do it early enough to take hold by the time it matters, but then you also have to get 'em where you're going. Honey's still alert when we get in the cab, the driver real hesitant to let us, but Bristol smooths it over, and then I really gotta urge her to get back out again, at an airfield. Not a lot of people around, that's good, and Bristol gives the driver a real good tip and I'm sure urges him to forget that he saw us. The standard.

As a team, we've only had a few helicopter rides together, but once Bristol's done something once, or studied it virtually with laser focus, she makes it look effortless forever after. She immediately greets Scooter and Meatball like they've been friends for years and sets them at ease, gets them talking about different things as they about fall over each other to stow her and Bits' gear. Butler helps me get Honey up into the chopper, and into the kennel that's strapped down and padded inside and honestly is probably the safest place on this whirlybird. Bristol's on a similar wavelength, I guess, 'cause she's got Meatball talking about the safety features, the ballistic parachutes that the thing has.

"Oh, don't *we* get parachutes?" she asks.

"No, that isn't how helicopters work," Scooter says. They look a little conflicted about whether to explain, or if it might be insulting, and Bristol just smiles graciously.

"I'm sorry, I didn't realize. Do forget I asked." She straps into one of the seats, accepts a headset. Our eyes meet briefly; yeah, this is gonna be her longest helicopter ride, and she wants to know what happens if the thing falls out of the sky. What we're supposed to do. I feel like I know, but not how to explain it in words. It's one of those trained things, and it'll kick in if I need it. I kinda shrug and flick my eyes to Bits and Bristol nods slightly. Bits can get her any intel she needs. We'll probably be over water for a lot of this; if we go down, I guess the chopper would float? I don't think normal ones would, but it seems like composite 3D printed ones would. Maybe we'll even have a shorter flight, less weight.

Honey's asleep before we're even in the air. I'm not sure yet who's piloting, Meatball or Scooter, but they take us up nice and easy, and I wonder where and how they got those chops, in addition to all the printing stuff. They've gotta be in their twenties. Good for them, really; we're all just making our way in the world. This is even legitimate. Or kind of. Legitimate enough that they're still getting flight clearance and operating in the open in Hong Kong.

I don't know if Butler was looking forward to around 12 hours of having me boxed in with him to converse or not, especially after I figure he's maybe the sniper from that night in Macau, but first order of business, really, is more shut-eye. Plus, the headsets aren't really noise canceling enough for good conversation. Bits could loop everybody in on our network and that might work out but, we'll worry about that when I wake up. Or nobody'll be worried and when I wake up it'll already be taken care of.

I don't know about anybody else, but I don't dream much. I did when I was little, I guess. Not so much after my experimental days. Maybe it's to do with them messing around with my programming. Maybe I'm just not super imaginative, who knows. Any time I try to remember when I sleep, it's mostly just maybe different colors, or if I'm warm enough. But nothing bothers me and I wake up good and refreshed, open my eyes to Butler asleep bolt upright, Bristol looking out the window, and Bits might've not moved the whole time.

"Where we at?" I ask.

"A few hours left," Bristol says. "Meatball mentioned not too long ago."

"So what do we do for the next eternity? Play I spy?" I lean a little, look out the window. "Whole lotta blue. Ooh a boat."

"*Please* no," Bristol says, turning her ever-suffering gaze to Butler, whose eyes are open now. "Why don't you tell us a story about how you and Dolly know each other?" Everybody just wants to know that, when we're out in the world, it's amazing.

"I promise, playing I spy's better." I laugh. "Anyway, Bristol, I already told you."

"Well you told me *your* version," Bristol says dismissively.

"Aw, I don't know," Butler says, with a play-bashful grin. He's never been bashful a day in his life. "We've always known each other."

"If you've always known each other, and are depriving me of a meet-cute, then can you tell me, has she always been like this?"

He's smiling and not lookin' at me and he says "Like what? A being of sweetness and light? Yup, that's our Dolly. Just the sweetheart of our town, she was, readin' library books to old folks and gettin' kittens out of trees."

"Aw come on, my reputation's gonna be ruined," I say.

"Dolly, your softer side is *hardly* a secret," Bristol says, a little smugly.

"Really? I thought I was still pretty intimidating. Obviously a hardened career criminal. A bloodthirsty, remorseless killer." I'm running out of descriptives.

"Maybe strangers think that, though I'm not sure how many acquaintances would say so."

"Well damn." I'm watching Bits, because I'm pretty sure she started paying attention to the real world a little while back and is just waiting for things to be safe before she takes her headset off. It's like how you can tell when somebody's pretend sleeping; after awhile you're just familiar enough with a person's breathing. And anyway, it's not like *she* knows what she breathes like when she's asleep or concentrating on virtual stuff. "I just feel so bad anytime anybody has the misfortune to be in my care."

"Nonsense darling," Bristol says briskly. "You've always done a marvelous job, so far as I'm aware."

"Well there was that time..." Butler says with a wicked grin, and I kick his foot.

"There's gotta be a first time for everything, okay? Plus you can hardly see the scar so I guess it turned out in the end." I don't know if you can hardly see the scar; I haven't seen him with his shirt off since we reunited.

"You simply *cannot* torture us like that," Bristol says. Bits sighs and pulls her VR goggles down around her neck, blinks around at us.

"You did fine taking care of me," she says, bless her heart. That ain't gonna be enough to distract Bristol.

"Thank you, Bits. See that's two outta three. Let's pray we don't need any more examples just now, huh?"

Bristol does pout now. "But I'm bored and want a story."

"Well you know what happened. After the..." Bits trails off, looking at Butler, who is listening with interest, realizes she doesn't really want to explain. "Anyway, it wasn't until then that I knew you knew how to cook, Dolly."

"I'm not certain you could call what Dolly does 'cooking,'" Bristol says delicately, and Butler laughs hard enough that Meatball turns around for a second. Good thing he seems to be the navigator and moral support.

"Aw come on, I make a perfectly serviceable steak with cast iron or a grill."

"A hubcap too, at least once," Butler says thoughtfully. He's like me, though, with a cast iron gullet. Like all of us are. Or were, I guess.

"A hubcap."

I grin. "Yeah, you know how it is. Sometimes circumstance makes it so you don't always have the right tools on hand."

"And...circumstance...led you to have steaks, but no appropriate means of cooking them."

"Well we *washed* the hubcap, if that's your problem." I watch her struggle, and I assume she decides against askin' after the provenance of the steaks.

"I don't think that's her problem, Dolly," Bits says helpfully.

"Yeah, prob'ly not." I grin at Bristol and she gives me her very small, very disapproving smile particularly crafted for moments like these, and Butler laughs again.

"So you three are a team?"

"We are business associates, yes," Bristol says primly.

"How's that work out for you."

I shrug. "Pretty good, mostly. We have our moments."

"Like stealin' a dog in one country that you had no plans to get to another?"

Bristol bites her lip. "We hit a snag."

"I should fucking say so." His tone is off, just a little.

"You don't need to be *crass* about it."

"....Crass?"

"She means the F word," I say, leaned over like I'm tellin' him a secret. He looks at me, and I wiggle my eyebrows at him. Is now the time to tell him I know? Nah.

"He can curse in other languages," Scooter interjects. We weren't disincludin' them on purpose, it's just hard when you're not lookin' at a person, even if everybody's in the headset.

"You don't understand, Bristol smells swear words." I look at the back of Scooter and they give me a thumbs up. "Plus, there's no telling what languages she knows. She picks them up like adaptive camouflage." And what a handy thing that lil proto-type adaptive camouflage box has been.

"I work very hard at it," she says.

"It's really impressive," Bits says, and Bristol looks pleased, so really, that's the best way this conversation could've turned, both me and Butler off the hotseat. For the moment. I'm sure the second I go find a bathroom or something once we're in Da Nang, she'll drag out his entire life story, and family history, and then mine, like how magicians pull knotted scarves outta their mouths. It's fine, it ain't new; I've resigned myself to my fate.

"Hey Meatball and Scooter, we're puttin' you up in a nice hotel, so you're nice and well rested for your flight back."

"Thanks!" Meatball says. Scooter nods in agreement, but yawns. I think they're the one that did the bulk of the flying and stuff.

"Not me?" Butler asks.

"Well I was under the impression you were interested in how this was gonna shake out," I say. "Or were you not?"

"Well I've got an interest," he says.

"I guess you might," I say, letting my tone slide a little off too, and he gets a little too still.

"Good, see, it's settled then," Bristol says. "It's possible we'll solve our little issue and we'll all be in the same hotel! Won't that be a treat, having a nice dinner together." Partway through that sentence, I see her rememberin' that nobody but her actually has nice dinner clothes, but to her credit, she soldiers on through to the end anyway.

"It'd be real keen," I say, grinning hard. "Lookin' forward to it."

"Real keen," Butler says slowly.

And it's banter all the way until landing, which really, there are worse ways to pass the time. It's been too long, since I've shared the same space with Butler for this long, and I'm not gonna be all starry-eyed about it. He's got more sense than to expect that, or he used to. After the job, though? We'll see how things play out. Especially after we talk about Macau, and his side jobs. Maybe the kind of rifle he's favoring lately. Business is business, he couldn't've known it was me, but I'm gonna let him squirm anyway.

Chapter Eighteen

======

Da Nang is dry and hot and I'm glad we aren't here for monsoon season, though I'm not sure which Bristol would find worse. She's the kinda person AC is made for. The airport's an airport, they're their own kind of places, y'know? Even walking off the tarmac from the helipad, we still gotta go through customs, and thank Christ Bits is as good as she is, we sail through no problem, everything stamped the way it needs to be, even the very sleepy dog's papers. She's a champ, though, just bumps into my leg as we walk, swinging her big head around to look at things.

Once we're outside again, Bristol immediately calling her new contact, mined from the old contact's phone, I just take a minute to look up at the night sky that we just came down from. We haven't been able to fly for all that long, people. It's kinda mind blowing when you think about it. Scooter looks a little nervous about leaving their helicopter, but I guess we arranged some kind of hangar and refuel for them, and they'll check it all over before they leave again tomorrow, so it's mostly the jitters from leaving a piece of equipment like that outta your sight. Plus they made every piece of it. That'll get you pretty attached.

Bristol drops her phone in her purse and looks off up the street. "Well?" I ask.

"He's at a hotel by the river, and after sitting for so long, I don't mind a walk. Shall we?"

"I think we'll find our own hotel, if you don't mind," Meatball says. "We're awfully tired after..."

"Oh I'm so sorry, what was I *thinking*? Bits, can you...?"

"On it," Bitsy says.

"I'll come along, if you don't mind," Butler says.

"Don't go thinkin' you get a cut," I say, grinning hard so he knows I really mean it.

"Nah, you already paid me. I just like seeing happy dog re-unions, my phone is full of 'em," he says, grinning so I can't tell if he's serious or not, and we both laugh. Bits looks at us kind of wide-eyed, like okay weirdos, and then looks at Meatball.

"You should be all set, the place is right that way."

"Thank you," he says, grinning but also suddenly shy, and I think oh Meatball honey, Bits isn't gonna be any kind of interested, just go to your hotel. But maybe I read it wrong, and him and Scooter are an item, it's not my business, and Scooter is in the jaw-cracking yawn stage of things, so now isn't the time to try and puzzle it out. They stumble-walk off on their way, though not with enough stumble that I think they need a minder.

Honey looks around at more and sniffs at more than in Macau, her ears canted forward, or at least I think they are. But she sniffs and sniffs, and sometimes stops to sniff with her nose up in the air, not on the ground, and I wonder what she's after, or thinks she's after. I wonder if dogs sometimes think they recognize a smell, the way us people think we recognize a person or a taste or a sound. Or a smell too, I guess, but dogs're way better at that. Bits told me once that smell-memories are the strongest ones, and I believe it. A certain smell'll take you back to school, or to your dad's garage when you were eight and holdin' the flashlight for him, or to picking blackberries in the summer with somebody who maybe-kinda wants to be your beau, while the cicadas scream in the trees all around you.

Bristol gives me a knowing look over her shoulder, she and Bits walking a little ahead. On purpose, I guess, to make sure me and Butler get time together. So obvious even I know what they're doing. Though I guess also I want to spend this last little time with the dog; we've only had her for a few days, but I guess she and I understand each other pretty well. We managed not to take any chunks out of each other, that's a pretty big deal. Wonder if Butler's still got that scar on his back, or if it got fixed with one of his upgrades. It wasn't on purpose. Maybe we're actually square by now, after everything.

"So in Macau…" Butler says, kinda guarded.

"Side job, I assume?"

"You're not pissed? I was already part broken down when I took my other shots, and—"

"You could've killed me," I said. "Or Bits or Bristol."

"Well yeah, that's what I'm trying to apologize for, if you stop being an asshole about it."

"You did kill Bristol's contact."

"And I was supposed to get his electronics to figure out where that goddamn dog went." We stop walking a minute, look at each other.

"And?"

"And what?"

"You didn't get them. Did you still get paid?"

"Yeah I still got paid. Got over there, took his picture, said somebody rolled him while he was still warm, thinkin' he was drunk. Like I was going to try and track down a couple people I barely saw in the first place?" He's telling the truth, and talking faster than he normally would, and I think he's maybe just thankin' christ he didn't kill me. He never would've known. Maybe years from now, if news ever got back home. If he ever got back home.

"Well there, see?" I reach up, pat him on the cheek. "Coulda happened to anybody."

"Dolly..."

"Shut up about it, already? I'm feelin' magnanimous, givin' you a pass." I start walking again, and about five steps later he catches up again.

We're getting closer to the river, there's a nice breeze off of it, and that watery smell, and then Honey about yanks the leash out of my hand, hittin' the end of it for the first time in our association. I keep hold, but I'm surprised. She looks back at me like, what are you doing, why are you stopping me, and scrabbles a little on the pavement until I walk faster. Still not fast enough for her, but better. Up ahead, Bristol's already talking to a guy, but he isn't looking at her, he's looking at the dog, and he steps past her and crouches down and I take a chance and let go of the leash and she runs and piles right into his chest, wagging furiously, licking anything of him that she can reach. Hot dogs can't fake that reaction; Honey's his dog all right.

He wraps his arms around her, and then feels the leash and grasps it, and after a few awkward moments of the rest of us standin' around waiting, Honey calms down enough for him to get up again. He's got some tear tracks on his cheeks, and he doesn't bother to wipe 'em off; can't say as I blame him. "Thank you," he says to each of us, sincerely, looking us in the eye. "I don't know what we would have done without you. We would never have been able to find her."

"You're welcome," I say, just as sincerely, and Bits kinda nods, and I can see Bristol's surprise and disappointment, see her gears turning, can see the image of flyin' away dollar signs in her eyes. I'm tryin' to figure a way to beam my thoughts into that pretty head of hers when she seems to come to a conclusion and smiles.

"It was our pleasure," she says warmly. "If you ever find yourself in such a difficulty again, or your associates, do please call us. We'll see what we can do about it."

//Guess we're not getting paid// Bits texts me morosely, or maybe she's just trying to head me off from sayin' something real stupid. I catch her eye and nod. Really, I'm just trying not to laugh, now. It's honestly kind of funny. We can't possibly demand this guy pay us. This guy might not be able to pay us. Probably, there was never any three million dollars. Well we got that one and a half mil, however they scraped that together. And you know, that's fine. That's enough, for the look on that guy's face, and the look on the dog's face. I'm gettin' soft, must be. I hand him the bag of her gear, if it is even her gear actually or just what whoever stole her was using, and he says thank you again. He seems more than a little disbelieving. That it's really his dog. That we're really just giving her back. But just like that, we're walking away in one direction, and he's goin' back to his hotel. //If we got upset about it, there's a guy with a rifle in that window there. Not a sniper rifle, I don't know how well it would have worked but...//

//But they tried to have insurance, in case we were real hardcore mercenaries.//

//Exactly.//

//Good thing for them we aren't.//

//Sure is.// I get a glimpse of her face; she's smiling like she isn't sure if she should be.

Bristol marches us right to an outdoor cafe there under the starlight, well the city lights, but the stars gotta be up there someplace. She stares at a menu that I'm not confident she can read and then she orders so I guess I'm wrong again, and then she looks out over the water in silence for a long time. Butler reaches for my hand under the table, and I let him. His skin is warmer than mine at first, and then after awhile, our hands match temperature.

"Hey Bristol," I say, after the guy brings us drinks, and a plate of spring rolls, and a basket of what I think are snails.

"Dolly," she says, blinking at the water and then looking over at me with maybe the saddest smile I ever saw on her face. "Do you ever just want to feel *nice*?"

"Well yeah, I guess I do," I say, both 'cause it's true and because it's the only thing to say to her right now.

Bits picks up her drink; it looks like we have glasses, but they're actually all plastic, probably safest by the river and on the pavement here, and we clunk them all together in a rattling toast, smiling cautiously at first and then broader, like the end scene in a wholesome 1900s sitcom. Maybe there's scales we all think about balancing, sooner or later. But yeah. It really is good, sometimes, to just feel nice.

Epilogue

Butler comes with me to Chiba, and we shack up at a hotel we pick at random in center city. A 7-Eleven is practically in view from our room window, and I can only kinda explain why I think that's funny. Or I can explain, he just doesn't get it, and that's fine. We're there three days, just gettin' room service and spending time making up for lost time, and on the morning of the fourth day, I get the message that my robot dog is ready.

I get dressed, quiet, and leave a note on hotel stationery. I'll be back, probably. Unless the devil takes me once I'm out in the street again. Pretty sure I don't have the heart for that, though, even if he did kinda wing me in Macau. Other'n if it's like, the end of war movie, and me going and doing whatever solo is what saves everybody. Even if I don't come back. I wonder how many goodbyes like that Bristol has pulled, just a note, maybe a *perfumed* note, I'd never think of that but she's so details-oriented, and then she's just a memory. Maybe zero. Maybe plenty. It's always hard to tell with her, always about appearances, and you gotta figure out what the reality of the situation is. I guess that's true of all of us.

They bring out the case with the white service tag still on the handle, but open it on the counter so that I can see proof of workmanship. I take the dog out of the case, crouch down and set it on the floor before I power it up. I almost feel like I cheated on it, goin' to play with a real dog while it was in the shop. The lights all come up, and it runs its usual boot sequence with wagging and head shaking, and it does a cute thing where it sits and lifts up a paw for you to shake. Then it's fully booted and it blinks at me, and starts wagging again, all on its own.

Jennifer R. Donohue grew up at the Jersey Shore and now lives in central New York with her husband and their Doberman. Though she got a bachelor's degree in psychology, she has always wanted to write. She currently works at her local public library, where she also facilitates a writing workshop. Her work has appeared in Daily Science Fiction, Syntax & Salt, Escape Pod, Truancy, DreamForge and elsewhere. She blogs at Authorized Musings, where she shares fiction and the tribulations of the writing life, and tweets @AuthorizedMusin.